Laundry Lady's Love

Stone's Creek
Ladies of Sanctuary House 1

Sophie Dawson

May your life be a story in faithful living.

~~~~~

Dedication

There is one person who has supported and encouraged me throughout my writing career. I've dedicated a book to him before but felt compelled to do so again. From our first communication within a writer's forum, we clicked. We've become siblings in the Lord and laughed and cried together as challenges and triumphs were shared. So again, I dedicate this book to you, George McVey who goes by the acronym PG, for Pastor George. Bless you. Thank you for being my mentor, encourager, and friend.

Acknowledgements

Whenever I come to acknowledging those who helped with one of my books, I have a difficult time choosing. How does one give thanks and honor to all who took the journey of creation with me? I go over in my mind all those involved and try to think of those whom I haven't mentioned in the past. This time I'm going to acknowledge my dedicated team of editors and beta readers. They enthusiastically take my draft and pick it apart to find the flaws so I can make it better. They find the typos, poor grammar, and punctuation marking up the file with red ink. And so, I honor Carolyn, Joy, Linda, Ruth, Cindy, and Angie. Thank you so very much.

Disclaimer

This is a work of fiction. Most of the places within the story are fictitious, but some are real. You will most likely recognize those which are. Those you don't are made up by me. The people, unless you recognize the name of a real historical person, are not real. They, too, have been created by me or by my friend and author George McVey. This is true of Nugget Nate and Penny Ryder, who may or may not show up in this book. Even if real historical people are mentioned, their lives may or may not adhere strictly to documented historical reference. In other words, what they do or say has little bearing in fact and they probably didn't do or say it. This is a fictional story after all.

All Scripture is quoted from the World English Bible.

Description

One man wants her, but the one she wants doesn't seem to.

Laura Duffle has come to Stones Creek, with her two young sons, hoping to find love again. She's spent the last five years at Sanctuary Place Mission for Women after the death of her husband. She needs to set up her laundry business but doesn't know where to start.

Hank Johnson, the town barber, is flattered by and attracted to the lovely widow who comes seeking his advice. He hasn't been looking for a wife, but maybe he'll begin with Laura.

Ranch foreman, Red Dickerson, would like a wife. He hopes to find one among the Ladies of Sanctuary House. He sets his sights on Laura.

Hank sets her heart on fire, but is he only interested in helping her get her business off the ground?

Red is solid and dependable, but is this enough to base her future on?

Should Laura settle for safety and security for herself and her boys?

Will she hold out for love?

Or will she just chuck both of them into the washtub and rinse the men from her life altogether?

Stones Creek Series
Ladies of Sanctuary House Character List

With the growth of Stones Creek and the many people who live there, I've decided a list of the main characters might be of interest and beneficial to the reader. Only the major characters are listed. This list includes those who appear in the Stones Creek. Children's ages reflect their age at the end of the book.

Sanctuary House Ladies and their children.

Blanche Basking
    Oswald Basking (Ozzie) - Blanche's son 13
    William Basking (Will) - Blanche's son 11
    Nancy Basking - Blanche's daughter 8
    John Basking - Blanche's son 6
Laura Duffle
    Edward Duffle (Eddie) - Laura's son 9
    Mark Duffle - Laura's son 7
Ruth Naylor
    Kathryn Naylor - Ruth's daughter 12
Cora Sepal
    Susan Sepal - Cora's daughter 3
Libby Trembly
Gema Volkovichna

~~~

Other Main Characters
Hank Johnson - Barber
Reddington Dickerson (Red) - Foreman of Hawk's Wing Ranch
Noah Preston - Preacher, Gunsmith
Hawk Conner - Owner Hawk's Wing Ranch
Lucy Tanner
Jack Tanner 16 months
Arleta Tanner 16 months

Stones Creek residents
Eli Steele - Doctor in Stones Creek
Leah Steele - wife to Eli
Lincoln Pierce (Linc) - Foreman of Chasing R Ranch
Elenora Pierce (Norie) - Linc's wife, daughter of Wes Chase, owner of Chasing R Ranch
Wesley Chase (Wes) - Owner of Chasing R Ranch, Norie's father
Ben Cutler - Owner of Cutler's General Store
Sara Cutler - Ben's wife
Seth Cutler - Son of Ben and Sara 10
Abigail Cutler (Abby) - Daughter of Ben and Sara 8
Clayton Cutler - Son of Ben and Sara 3
Newt Riverby - Sheriff
Myra Riverby - Sheriff Newt's wife
Troy Hope - Myra's son 5
McIlroy - Blacksmith
Chloe McIlroy
Duncan Ashburn (Dunc) - Chloe's Son 14
Penelope Ashburn (Lil-Pen) - Chloe's daughter 5
Dak Levine - Deputy

Cora Levine - Dak's wife

Susan 3

Thomas Wilson - Ex-slave

Almeda Wilson - Ex-slave, Thomas's wife

Spike Hunter - Sablemaster on Chasing R Ranch

Doris Hunter - Housekeeper on Chasing R Ranch, Spike's wife

Vernie Preston - Noah Preston's wife

Nugget Nate Ryder - Uncle of Ben Cutler

Penny Ryder - Nate's wife

Garfield Steele - Eli's father

Chalmers Jehosaphat Ritter (C.J.) - Banker

Arty Massot - Carpenter

CHAPTER ONE

Laura Duffle stood in front of the barber shop and waited for the man leaning his chair back against the building to acknowledge her. His Stetson shaded his face so she couldn't see what he looked like. At least not his eyes. His face was clean shaven, his chin square. When he didn't move, she decided to address him.

"Excuse me, Mr. Johnson. Might I have a moment of your time?"

The chair slowly tipped down to rest on all four legs. The man rose to stand before her. He lifted the hat from his head. "Ma'am. What can I help you with?"

Now she could see that his hair was a dusty shade of blonde. Not dusty as unclean, but rather the color of the dirt street. His handsome face looked to be just a few years older than Laura's twenty-seven years. His eyes were deep brown and focused on her with an intensity that made her pulse quicken.

"My name's Laura Duffle, and I'm new in town. I'm looking to start a laundry service here in Stones Creek. Since mainly men will need my services and your customers are men, I was wondering if you'd be so kind as to spread the word? I'm experienced at doing laundry for hire and pretty fast. I'd be much obliged to you. If you'd help me." The words tumbled so quickly out of her mouth she wondered if he would be able to understand them.

"I'd be happy to help you, Miss Duffle."

"Actually, it's Mrs. Duffle. I'm widowed."

That fact must have surprised him as his eyes widened just a bit. It was a common misconception about the women who had come so recently to Stones Creek. Many had never been married even though they had children. Several were ex-prostitutes or other forms of kept women. However, Laura had been spared that sort of degradation.

Her husband, Alan, had died leaving her with very little to support her, and her two sons. He'd been gone five years. Eddie was now nine, and Mark had recently turned seven. She'd been fortunate that Nugget Nate Ryder had answered one of his Callin's and found her as she tried to find honest work in the Illinois town they'd been traveling through when her husband died.

Nate had gathered the grieving family and taken them to Sanctuary Place in Iowa. The Place was his mission for abused, abandoned and destitute women. She had never heard the tale of why he'd set the mission up. She was just thankful that he had. Without Nate's mission, Laura might have had to resort to selling herself to provide for her sons.

"Can you give me a few more details about your business? How much you charge? The time it will take for you to finish? Where you plan to do the work?"

"Oh, I hadn't thought about how much to charge. What do you think?"

"I thought you said you'd done laundry for hire before. What did you charge then?" Mr. Johnson eyed her with mild suspicion.

Heat flamed Laura's face. How could she not have thought about what to charge? It was such a basic question. "Well, um. I may have fudged that a bit. I did do laundry for other people, but it was more a barter type arrangement. At Sanctuary Place, we traded labor or labor for items. I've never actually charged money for my work. What do you think would be a fair price?"

The man looked at her for a long moment. "How's about I bring out another chair, and we palaver about your venture in comfort?"

"That'd be just fine, Mr. Johnson." A grateful smile bloomed on her face.

He brought another chair from the shop and placed it catty corner to the one she sat in. "You tell me about this laundry business you're wanting to start. I'll help you work out the details."

They spent the next half hour or so discussing Laura's plans and refining them. There were so many things she had never thought about that Mr. Johnson brought to her attention. As a thank you for all his help, Laura offered to do his first load of laundry for free.

"That about covers everything I can think of right now," the barber said. "I'll gather up my laundry and have it ready for tomorrow. You don't have to do it for free. I'll pay you."

"Oh, I want to do this batch for you, no charge. That way you will be able to recommend me. It's also a way for me to pay you back for the advice and the advertising you will do for me. For that sign, you said you'd make, too. I truly appreciate it."

"Not a problem, ma'am. Having a pretty little lady like you working near the back of my shop will bring customers into it."

The compliment made Laura blush. Praise in any form had been few and far between since her husband died.

"Well, I won't take any more of your time. I'll be coming for the laundry about eight-thirty tomorrow morning." She stood up, and when he did too, she held out her hand. He took it and gave it a gentle shake. "Thank you, again. Have a good day, Mr. Johnson."

"Since we'll be working rather closely together, how's about you just call me Hank." The man gave her a wide smile. It seemed innocent enough. A bit familiar for their short acquaintance, but she felt comfortable with him after all their discussion.

"Thank you, Hank. You may call me Laura."

Laura's heart was beating hard as she walked away. She'd done it. She'd negotiated with the barber to advertise her laundry business. He wanted her to do his laundry, so she had her first customer. Granted, she was doing his first batch for free, but it would be worth it since he was going to spread the word to his customers so they could become hers, too.

At supper that evening, she told everyone at Sanctuary House about her venture. The eight women and their children had arrived the previous week in Stones Creek. They had come from Sanctuary Place Mission for Women in Iowa to the small Colorado town to possibly become brides for the men of the area.

Until they married, the women were to develop businesses or take employment to support themselves and their children. It was why Laura was starting her laundry service.

"I'll stop at Cutler's General Store in the morning and purchase my laundry soap. I appreciate you all letting me use a couple of the laundry tubs for my business until I can afford to get my own."

"We'll make sure you have what you need until you can buy them," Blanche Basking, the unofficial head of the House, said. "We have to support each other in our ventures."

"Thank you. I am going to talk with Hank about the price since we didn't figure in firewood. I may need to increase it to cover that cost. I do like the idea of having the older boys supply me with the wood. It's a way they can earn some money."

"Hank, huh? You're on a first name basis with him?" Ruth Naylor asked with a grin.

Heat flushed Laura's cheeks. "He asked me to call him that, so I thought it was polite to reciprocate."

~~~~~

Hank took the extra chair back into his shop and set it next to another one by the window. It wasn't often that he needed to have the extra chairs, but occasionally several cowboys came to town at the same time, and all wanted haircuts. A few times he'd even had his two bathing rooms full as well.

There was a well pump behind the shop that serviced both the building he was in, with the bakery on one side and the gun shop on the other, and Sanctuary House behind. The town was fortunate to sit over a fairly shallow aquifer, and several wells had been dug shortly after the town was started.

Hank had an indoor cistern he filled daily so he wouldn't have to stop cutting hair when someone wanted to take a bath. It was attached to a stove to heat the water. He wondered how Laura would draw and heat her water. Laundry took a lot of water. Hot water. He'd have to investigate. Maybe there was some way he could make it easier for her.

Just why he was interested in helping her quite so much, he didn't know. Well, maybe he did. It was too early to start courting. There couldn't be any done for a month after they arrived. They still had about three weeks to go.

He was helping Laura start her laundry business, not court her. Hank smiled. It couldn't hurt to assist her, and it gave him a leg up on getting acquainted.

Hank went back to sitting in the July sun with his hat over his eyes. Slow day. Not surprising in that it was early in the week. Most of the cowboys didn't come for a shave and haircut until they got paid on Friday. They wanted to get cleaned up for their time at the saloon.

The thought of spending time and money there made Hank cringe. Not only was it expensive, but it also wasn't the way the Lord wanted a man to act. No, he'd save his money and body for a woman he'd marry. He had waited all these years, and he could do so for a while longer.

The image of Laura Duffle came to the forefront of his mind. She seemed like a sweet woman. Definitely not a business woman, at least not yet. He could help her with that.

Hank wondered whether she had children. That was something he'd need to know before he decided whether he wanted to court her or not.

Hank didn't know anything about children. Especially girls. He'd been the youngest of his family by eight years. His older brothers and sisters had left the house as he grew into his pre-teen years. Several had moved away. As the baby of the family, Hank knew he'd been spoiled. That was probably why he hadn't made it as a cowboy.

They had to work too hard. Up at dawn, wrangling cattle all day or fixing fences. Tending the horses and all that tack. Being outside in all sorts of bad weather. Nope, just didn't fit the way he wanted to live his life. Barbering and the bathhouse worked well for him. Good honest work, easy work, but profitable.

A laundry lady would fit well into his life. He didn't like

doing all the towels his business generated. He'd pay for it to be done. Might even be able to wrangle a discount if he could figure out how to offer her something in return. Time and watching her do the job would answer that.

The sound of heeled boots coming towards him sounded along the boardwalk. Hank lifted his Stetson and saw Sheriff Newt Riverby approach.

"Afternoon, Hank. Looks like I came at a good time for a shave and haircut."

"You did at that. Come on in." Hank stood and opened the door allowing the sheriff to proceed him in.

CHAPTER TWO

Laura finished her kitchen duties the next morning and made sure Eddie and Mark had completed theirs. The boys each planned to play with other boys of the House, overseen by Ruth who was being paid to monitor their activities and tend the children while their mothers worked.

She hurried to Cutler's General Store and purchased two bars of laundry soap and a small knife to shave them into the water. She inquired about the cost of wash tubs and planned to ask Hank how long he thought it might take for her to earn enough to purchase them.

When she arrived at the barbershop, Laura was surprised it wasn't open yet. After all, it was already after eight in the morning.

Deciding she could get some washing done, Laura went back to the House and gathered up the towels and the napkins from breakfast. With the number of people living there, a lot of dirty laundry was produced, so she took what was piled in the baskets in the washroom. Trading her service for fewer chores in the House was part of the barter system the ladies had brought with them from Iowa.

A fire was built in the backyard with a wrought iron stand for the wash water. Laura began her routine of pumping water and filling the large kettles. She was well into the job, hanging the first items on the clotheslines, when a male voice asked, "Weren't you going to commence doing my laundry today?"

She looked behind her to find Hank standing with a pile of laundry in his arms. Eyeing him, she said, "I came to get the things as soon as breakfast was finished. You were not in evidence yet. Not wanting to waste my day waiting, I started on these things." Laura waved her hand at the line nearly full of clean linens from the House.

A redness tinged his face. She fought back a smile. Men! They thought a woman should be at their beck and call at all times.

"Yes, well... I brought my laundry to you."

"Thank you. I was going to come for it once I got the rest of this load hung up. Set them on that bench, please. I'll bring them back this afternoon."

Hank did as he'd been told, then stood watching her. It made Laura nervous. No man, not even her husband, had ever spent time observing her do laundry.

"Um, do you need anything else?" She didn't like that her words sounded tentative.

"Oh, no. I don't suppose so. I'll get that sign made for my window this morning. Should finish it and get it posted once the paint dries. I found a piece of wood to use that I can paint." Hank shuffled his feet.

It struck Laura that he was just as nervous as she was. Pausing after she pinned a small shirt on the line, she stepped away from the basket and approached him.

"Thank you for bringing your laundry. I could have come for it."

Hank cleared his throat. "I should have remembered you said you'd set about early. I've heard you ladies and all, up before I generally am. I, um, live above the shop."

"Oh." She didn't know how to respond. It seemed so personal to know he could hear the activity of the House from his living quarters.

"Next time, I'll make sure to have the bundle to you early." Hank turned to leave.

"Um, Hank." Laura stepped forward. "It wasn't really a problem. Also, I need your advice again." She went on to explain about the need for wood for the fire and her thoughts about paying some of the boys to gather and chop for her. "Do you think what I plan to charge will be enough so I can make a profit?"

"Might be tight for a while, until you get a clientele built up, but should work out." Hank rubbed a hand across his chin.

"Oh, good. I was afraid I'd have to raise the rates before I even started." She smiled at him. He didn't have his hat on so she could see that his dark blonde hair was somewhat curly even though it was cut short. A thought struck her. "Hank," she said. "Who cuts your hair? You're the barber."

He grinned at her, a dimple appearing in his chin. His straight white teeth gleaming in the morning sunshine contrasted with his dark brown eyes. "I do. It's something the man who trained me taught me how to do. Takes time to learn how to cut looking in a mirror. I'm much better at it now."

Laura surveyed his head. "You'll do. A fine advertisement for your shop." She stepped back toward the clothesline and basket of wet laundry waiting to be hung, signaling an end to the conversation. He was a handsome man, and she didn't need the distraction.

~~~~~

Hank watched her lean over to pick up a wet garment,

straightening and lifting her arms to pin it to the line. She was a mighty fine looking woman. Her Mother Hubbard dress of brown and red striped cotton hid most of her curves, but she was slim in the right places and full in the ones that interested a man. She'd unbuttoned the cuffs and rolled her sleeves back, exposing her forearms. Her bonnet shielded her face from his view, but he knew how pretty she was.

When she didn't come to the shop to collect his dirty laundry, he'd been a bit peeved. Laura had said she'd come first thing in the morning. When he'd exited the back door, his irritation had turned to himself. She'd obviously been working for quite a while. The clothesline was half filled and would be totally soon with the rest of the load waiting to be hung. It made him somewhat ashamed that he'd not been up and ready with his laundry when she had come to the shop.

Maybe he needed to be open earlier in the morning. That hadn't seemed necessary since most of his customers came later in the morning or after lunch. Of course, with the ladies of Sanctuary House waiting to be courted, he'd most likely see more men wanting shaves, haircuts, and baths.

That thought pleased him. It meant more income, something that was always welcome.

Hank turned away from the pleasing view of the young woman and crossed the alley, going in the back door of his shop. He had a sign to paint, as well as changing the opening time for his shop.

~~~~~

Laura walked along the boardwalk and peeked into the barbershop through the large window. She didn't want to disturb Hank if he were with a customer. Most of the laundry Hank had brought her that morning was folded into the pillowcase he'd included. She'd done the sheets and towels first figuring he'd need those back as soon as possible. The towels he needed for his work and the sheets were, most likely, the only set he had.

Laura studied the room. Against the wall was an oak shelving unit. In the center was a large mirror. The cabinet base was deeper on the sides than in the middle. She figured that was so Hank could move easily between it and the barber chair.

Never having seen one before, Laura was surprised that the chair simply looked like an armchair with a headrest and attached foot stool. On the opposite wall near the door was a row of hooks attached to a board. Several chairs were lined up under the window. A doorway covered with a curtain must lead to a hall where the bathing rooms would be located.

A man was putting money on the counter while Hank swept up hair on the floor. They were chatting and laughing. Shortly, the man moved to the door and took his hat off the hook, so Laura walked over. As he exited, he looked Laura up and down, a smile spreading across his face.

"Ma'am." He tipped his hat. "I'm Red Dickerson, cowboy on the Bent Arrow Ranch. Pleased to make your acquaintance. I'll get an introduction at the school raising." Red smiled and ambled across the boardwalk, jumped down to the street, and slipped under the hitching rail. Taking the horse's reins, he mounted, tipped his hat again, and set the horse in motion to head out of town.

Laura stood watching until he kicked the horse into a gallop. She took in a deep breath of air and slowly let it out. No man had looked at her in such an intense way since her husband, Alan. Oh, my.

Turning, she met the gaze of Hank. He was looking at her,

too. Just as intently. Laura swallowed. Pasting a smile on her face, she held out the pillowcase filled with clean laundry. "I've brought part of what you gave me this morning. The rest still needs to be ironed. I thought you might need the towels and …" She paused. Sheets were such an intimate thing. "These." It was a lame finish, but all she could muster in the situation. She pulled her lips into some semblance of a smile.

Hank took the bundle. "Thank you. I appreciate you thinking of the towels. I've been busier than I thought I'd be today. I'm a thinking it's the school raising. Men are wanting to gussy up for when they meet you ladies."

Laura couldn't help but glance where the cowboy had disappeared.

"Would you please come and look at the sign I painted for you? I think you'll be tickled with it." Hank stood back and held out an arm to indicate she should precede him into the barbershop.

The room was well lit by the large window. There were lamps fixed to the wall. It was neat, but a pile of towels had been tossed on the floor in the corner. The barber chair was centered before the mirror. A potbellied stove was against the back wall with a large tank attached to it.

Leaning on the counter was a small sign:

Duffle Laundry Service

One to Four Day Service Available

Prices Negotiated

"Um, I thought it might be best to be vague about the cost. Also, the time. That way, if you're busy you can charge a bit more if they want it back right quick."

"What a wonderful idea. I would have never thought of that. I was worried about being able to get everything done if I had a lot of customers all at one time."

Hank smiled. "Glad you like it. I was a mite concerned you'd think I was being pushy."

"No, thank you. I appreciate your talent for business." Laura reached out her hand and placed it on his arm, emphasizing her words.

Hank stood just a bit taller. He cleared his throat. "Would you like to see the rest of the shop? I had another thought, too."

"Certainly."

As he led the way through a curtained doorway, into a hall, Hank said, "I thought, maybe, I would put a basket back here." He pointed to the floor next to the back door. "I could put the laundry in it, and you could fetch it up without going around the building. It'd save you a heap of steps. Since you'll be doing the towels mighty often, it'd add up over time."

Laura grinned. "Thank you. I could deliver the clean things back here, too. Just place them in the basket. That way I won't be disturbing you and your customers."

The look Hank gave her made butterflies dance in her stomach. "Mrs. Duffle, Laura, you could never disturb me with your presence."

Oh, my.

~~~~~

That evening Laura carried her Bible down to the parlor. It was the room across the foyer from the dining room on the first floor. It was large enough for the ladies to gather with a few others. There were several settees and straight chairs as well as occasional tables. Sconces on the walls as well as table lamps could be lit to illuminate the room. There weren't a lot of knick-knacks as the ladies hadn't had them to bring. A couple of the chairs now had tatted doilies. More would appear as they were completed. Ruth tatted well, and Esther could crochet with the thinnest of threads. Laura knit and crocheted but only practical items such as socks, mittens, hats, and scarves.

Laura turned the wick up in the oil lantern sitting on a table by the settee. It was her favorite of the lamps because the base was beaded swirls in red glass. She'd just settled the boys in bed. The evening light was fading to darkness. She was tired but wanted a bit of time with the Lord.

The bookmark took her to where she'd last left off reading — Jeremiah twenty-nine. When she came to verse eleven, Laura ran her finger over the words. *For I know the plans I have for you, says the Lord, plans for your welfare, and not for evil, to give you a future and a hope.*

God did have a plan for Laura's future. It was something she'd doubted when her husband died, and she couldn't find honest work. Just when Laura thought she would have to resort to the oldest profession, God had provided for her.

Laura had been expecting when they left Pennsylvania but lost the baby as they traveled through Indiana. Then Alan had died in a small town in Illinois. There hadn't been any opportunities for employment there, and Laura had struggled to get the oxen moving to pull the wagon to the next town.

That's where Nugget Nate had shown up. The tall, buckskin clad man was standing in the middle of the street when Laura came out of the mercantile nearly in tears. She was exhausted, holding the hand of almost four-year-old Eddie and carrying eighteen-month-old Mark. The woman she had spoken to in the store had looked at her with a haughty expression and told her the only employment for her kind was at the brothel just outside of town. That the woman hadn't known Laura from Adam didn't seem to matter. The assumption that she was a fallen woman stung. Laura hadn't known what to do. Just as the tears started to fall, she heard a deep male voice.

"You's be a lookin' like you's in need of some help, ma'am. I do believe I be the one who been called ta help ya." The man strode up the street with long steps and picked up Eddie, tossing him in the air, catching him easily to his chest. "Mighty fine young 'un ya got here, ma'am. That un, too. My Penny'll be pleased ta have 'em ta tend to whilst we make our way ta Sanctuary Place."

"Sir, um. I'm not that kind of woman. I'm a God-fearing person and won't be selling myself..."

The man began to laugh, then stopped abruptly and gave her a fierce look. "Ain't never in my life been ta that kind o' woman and never made a lady into one. Rescued a few and that's what I'm a doin' now. Keepin' ya from havin' ta make the choice to eat or not. God done give ya them two little ones. He ain't wantin' ya to have ta sin in order ta be a keepin' em fit and a growin'.

"Name's Nugget Nate Ryder, an' my wagon an' wife, Penny, be at the edge of town a waitin' on my figurin' out what the Callin' done brung us here fer. Now that I done that, it be time ta skedaddle outa here. That there be yer wagon?"

He lifted Eddie's arm to point. Eddie giggled. It was the first time since Alan died that his son had laughed. The tightness and fear in Laura's heart eased. It seemed as if God had heard her prayers after all.

She'd felt so abandoned by God in the past few weeks. First, losing her little girl who'd been born far too early. Then, Alan dying of a fever just a few days ago. Having to leave both graves, never to visit again. Not being able to find honest work in either town. Thinking she'd have to take employment in a saloon or brothel to be able to feed her sons. She'd cried out to her Heavenly Father but hadn't seemed to be on the receiving end of His blessing and provision.

Now, the famous Nugget Nate Ryder, legendary, wealthy, mountain man of the West, defender of the victimized, and purveyor of justice stood before her. God hadn't forgotten her. Hadn't ignored her pleas. He had sent Nugget Nate to help her in her hour of desperation.

Tears had fallen down Laura's face, and she nearly collapsed in relief. God had provided. "Praise be to God. You, sir, are an answer to prayer. My faith is restored."

Without saying another word, which Laura would later find out was very unusual for Nugget Nate, he led her to her wagon and helped her and the boys settle onto the seat. He climbed up beside them and with a "Hup!" set the oxen on their plodding way to the edge of town where Penny, the love of his life, waited.

Since that time, Laura held to the promise of that verse in Jeremiah. God did have a plan for her life and that of her boys. It was what had prompted her to choose to come to Stones Creek with the first group of ladies from the Place. As insecure as Laura had been about the move, she'd wanted more than living at the mission for herself, for her sons too. The possibility of her marrying again, and thus the benefits of having a father help rear them into manhood, was what she hoped was God's plan for her life.

Now, Laura had the beginnings of a business which could sustain her if, and until she chose to marry. Laura knew about laundry. She'd been doing it for the last five years at Sanctuary Place.

Laura had a Daguerreotype of herself and Alan taken at the time they were married. In its hinged case, the image sat on her bedside table. With the possibility of a suitor, maybe she should close the case and put the image away. Not yet though. It still gave her comfort to look at his handsome face. Mark was looking more like him all the time. Neither boy remembered their father. They'd been too young when he died.

Laura read the verse again. Yes, she'd stand on that promise. God did have a plan for her. She just needed to be willing to keep focused on His plan and not go heading off in a different direction.

CHAPTER THREE

Laura accepted another coffee mug and dipped it in the dishwater. It might have been the hundredth one she washed that day. The people of Stones Creek were raising the school building. People, mostly men of course, had come from around the area to help with its construction. There was the ulterior motive of meeting the women who had come to town and were living at Sanctuary House.

The scarcity of women in the West and eight single women suddenly in town drew interested men from a wide area. That the women were fairly young and willing to marry peaked that interest. Few of the men cared that most had rather unsavory pasts. Now, however, the women were all Christian believers and looking for a better future for themselves and their children.

Laura's past wasn't something to regret. She'd simply been unfortunate to have her husband die as they migrated from Pennsylvania, heading west looking for more opportunity than they'd had back home.

The late July day was sunny but not overly hot. There was enough of a breeze to keep the insects from pestering. It came down from the mountains to the west and brought the scent of pine and honeysuckle with it.

A whistle cut through the air calling attention to a good looking young man standing on the bed of a buckboard wagon. He'd been introduced to Laura earlier as Lincoln Pierce. He was the foreman of the Chasing R Ranch and married to the owner's daughter.

"I've been asked to make an announcement as my voice carries well."

"Some might call you a loudmouth," another voice yelled from the crowd. Laughter erupted. Linc chuckled, too.

"Suppose so, but if you want to be introduced to the ladies, you might want to be nice to me, Pete." Another round of laughter made the man pause. "As you all know, Stones Creek has been blessed by the arrival of eight beautiful women along with their children.

"Nugget Nate made it possible for these women to come and find new homes and lives here. They are willing to consider marrying. One of the objectives of today is to introduce them. Now, I'm not going to haul them up into the wagon so you can view them. They aren't cattle.

"Many of you have met them as they've gone about town. They've begun to make changes, additions to Stones Creek. The Creek Cafe has opened, adding to Mrs. Wilson's bakery. There's a new dressmaker in with Mrs. Steele. Many of you are much less scruffy now that Mrs. Duffle is available to wash your clothing."

Laura blushed at being mentioned. Her business was doing well. The first couple of weeks had been rough. Many of the men who employed her to do their laundry hadn't had their clothing washed in far too long. It made getting them clean take longer, with much more scrubbing. She'd raised her fees for the initial washing to reflect that. Although the men grumbled some, they agreed and paid. She'd made it clear that if they waited until their clothes were that dirty again, she would charge even more.

Telling the men had taken all the courage she had, but once she'd instructed several men, it got easier. She wasn't going to allow herself to be overworked per load just because someone didn't want to have their clothing washed often enough. Hank had praised her for her steadfast insistence, telling her she was getting to be a dab hand at business. His comment had raised her spirits after a particularly trying day.

Linc went on, explaining how the courting of the women would be handled. Four respected men of the community had been tasked with overseeing that the women were courted and could choose who would be allowed to court them. Each man had to gain the approval of these men: Dr. Eli Steele, Ben Cutler, the general store owner, Sheriff Newt Riverby, and Pastor Noah Preston.

Today, any man could be introduced, and that was encouraged, but if they were interested in doing any courting, they needed to speak with the men in charge.

The thought of meeting all the men gathered for the school raising made Laura's stomach clench. She'd known Alan since they were young. They'd courted while she finished school, then gotten married. She'd had Eddie a year and a half later, and Mark two years after that.

Linc, jumping down from the wagon, brought Laura's thoughts back to the present. People began mingling again, and Ruth handed her another dirty coffee mug. Well, she wouldn't meet very many of the men standing behind the tub of dishwater.

Surveying the area showed piles of lumber and tools. The foundation and floor had been built previously. Walls and the roof would be erected today. If all went well, the building would be framed, shingled, and sided by nightfall. Several men were already carrying boards and beginning to nail them together.

"Laura, Ruth," Mrs. Sara Cutler said, walking up to them. "Let Mrs. Fugard and me take over the washing. We want you to go and be introduced to the community, don't we, Mrs. Fugard?"

The pinched look on the woman's face said just the opposite. Laura and the rest of the House ladies knew Mrs. Fugard didn't approve of them coming to Stones Creek. Most of the people welcomed the addition to the town. Of course, most were men who were hoping to find wives. Several of the women considered all the House ladies soiled doves, not worthy to walk on the same side of the street. Mrs. Fugard was one of them.

Laura smiled and wiped her hands on a damp dish towel. "Thank you, Mrs. Cutler, Mrs. Fugard. That's mighty obliging of you. I would like to get one of Mrs. Wilson's donuts before they're all gone. Wouldn't you, Ruth?"

Mrs. Fugard sniffed as she took the apron Ruth had removed. Laura handed hers to Mrs. Cutler, and they stepped away from the washing station toward the group of men and women milling around the school yard.

"Laura," Hank called as he stepped forward. "Would you please introduce me to your friend? I believe I've met all the ladies of the House except her."

His request took Laura by surprise. Not that he wanted to be introduced to Ruth, but how his interest in another woman made her feel. She realized she'd sort of assumed Hank the barber was kind of hers. The thought that he might be attracted to Ruth settled in her stomach like a burnt cup of coffee.

"Of course," Laura said, taking Ruth by the hand and drawing her toward the group Hank was standing in front of. "Mrs. Ruth Naylor, I'd like you to meet Mr. Hank Johnson. Mr. Johnson, this is Mrs. Ruth Naylor."

Hank tipped his hat and smiled. "Pleased to make your acquaintance."

"Likewise, I'm sure." Ruth's cheeks turned a pleasing shade of pink.

Laura swallowed, unease settling in her belly. She smoothed the front of her dress.

"Hank, my friend, how about you introducing both of these ladies to me?" The voice was that of Red Dickerson who had briefly made himself known to Laura at the barbershop the other day. He'd mentioned he would get an introduction at that time. Seems he was fulfilling that desire.

Red filled out his tan canvas trousers well. That his legs were strong was evident by the width of his thighs. He had on a dark green cotton shirt that stretched a bit across his chest. Just like most of the men, there was a holster, with a revolver, belted around his waist, and a cowboy hat on his head.

Hank turned, and Laura noted just a bit of a frown on his lips. It vanished in a moment, so maybe she was mistaken. Soon, the names were all exchanged, and Hank was smiling again.

"You mentioned the other day you worked on the Bent Arrow Ranch. Is that very far from town?" Laura asked.

"Not far. Spread starts a few miles south of here. Might be getting a name change soon though. Seems Mr. Mader, the owner, is in the midst of selling the place. His wife wants to move to Denver. They have a son and daughter who both live there. Son never wanted to ranch. He's some businessman there."

Then, they were surrounded by a large group of men. Each one wanted to be introduced, but also wanting to know about the ranch being sold. Many of the men Laura already knew. She was doing their laundry. Others were introduced to both ladies.

The men were varying in looks and age. Some were quite young, barely needing to shave. Others had gray at the temples or in their mustaches. They milled around, vying for attention.

The press of bodies surrounding Laura caused her palms to sweat. She rubbed them on her skirts trying to keep a pleasant expression on her face. Ruth seemed to be enjoying the attention. Laura needed to get out from the center of the crowd.

"Laura." It was Hank's voice. "I think Mark needs you. Come with me."

She jerked her head up, trying to see over the heads of the men. Where was her son? He needed her. Hank took hold of her hand and led her out of the group of men. They walked to the other side of the partially completed building. A number of children were playing there.

It looked to Laura as if they were playing blind man's bluff. Mark was in the middle of the pack, laughing and running.

"I don't think he needs me." She looked at Hank.

"Oh, I suppose not." He grinned down at her. "Maybe it was Mark's mother who needed a bit of help getting away from a herd of pestering men." He hadn't let go of her hand and gave it a gentle squeeze. Then, he released it. "Just wanted you to be comfortable. You seemed flusterated just now. Like you needed to get out of there."

Laura smiled up at him. "I did. Thank you."

"Anytime."

~~~~~

Hank was stropping his razor when the shop door opened, and McIlroy stepped in. Placing the blade on a folded towel on the counter, Hank said, "You finally come to get yourself presentable, McIlroy?"

The blacksmith nodded. "Yep, you think it's about time?"

Hank was glad he'd set the blade down, or he would have dropped it. He'd been teasing the shaggy blacksmith for years about getting his hair and beard under control. Hank thought McIlroy just hacked at both when he wanted to shorten the mess.

"Past time, if you ask me. Come on. Have a seat." Hank waved a hand at his barber chair. "What brought this fine thought to your head? Cain't be me. I've been bird-dogging you for months to darken my door."

"Gonna be doing some courting."

Hank's hands paused as he began brushing McIlroy's hair. He swallowed. "Who you plannin' on courting?"

"Mrs. Ashburn. She's got Dunc and Lil-Pen and is partnering with Almeda Wilson and Mrs. Basking in the cafe and bakery."

Something eased in Hank. He didn't want to think of Laura Duffle being courted by someone. Maybe he'd talk with Pastor Noah about it. Then again, it might be early days yet. It was a major consideration. He needed to be sure not to make any hasty decisions.

The women had only been here about six weeks. Hank had heard that Sheriff Riverby was interested in that little spitfire Myra Hope. His new deputy, Dak Levine, was openly courting Cora Sepal. Both women, as well as Chloe Ashburn, had children. That was the major stumbling block to Hank. He wasn't sure he wanted a ready-made family. Seemed like a lot of work to him. He just didn't know if it was worth it.

Sure, having a woman had definite advantages, chief among them were sharing a bed and the activities participated in there. Children normally followed in time. Taking on one or more children already living seemed a bit much to ask of a man.

Several of the women had only one child, but Mrs. Ashburn had two, and Mrs. Basking had four. Hank nearly shuddered at the thought of four children. Laura had the two boys. They were cute, and she was closer to his age than Mrs. Basking who he'd heard was in her middle thirties. Hank, being thirty-one, didn't think he wanted to marry an older woman. Besides, Mrs. Basking seemed to be the managing sort. She appeared to be the leader of the House. Hank might not be the most aggressive or motivated, but he wanted to be the head of his household.

"You're not very talkative today, Hank. You feelin' under the weather?" McIlroy asked.

Hank chuckled. "No, just concentrating on taming the beast that's springing forth from your head. All this hair I'm cutting off is going to fill my wastebasket."

Soon, Hank was sweeping up black clippings as McIlroy left the shop. When the floor was clean, he walked to the back of the shop and stood looking out the window in the door, and watched as Laura Duffle took laundry off the line, folding each piece, and laying it in the basket.

CHAPTER FOUR

Summer turned to autumn. In September, Birdie Pullman met and married rancher Harvey Hayes in the space of four days, becoming a mother to his three children. Esther Fuller suddenly married and left Stones Creek with Trapper Ted who she had known as a child.

Ruth came to stand next to Laura who was hanging clothing on the line. With most of the children in school, Ruth's child care duties had dwindled. She only had four little ones so consequently more time on her hands. Soon, there would be even fewer when Myra married Sheriff Newt, and Cora married Deputy Dak in early November. McIlroy had proposed to Chloe at the same time Newt had proposed to Myra. When all the weddings were over there would only be one House child and Almeda's baby boy for her to tend most of the time.

"Once Myra and Cora are married, I could move the cleaning jobs to the late afternoons. Blanche and Chloe are both home by then," Ruth said.

Laura pinned another pair of pants on the line. "Chloe will be leaving in December when she and McIlroy get married. I don't like you thinking of working at night. Being in the buildings alone, and walking through town in the dark to get home."

"I don't either, but what else can I do? I'm not making enough with only the four children and will make even less when I only have two, Blanche's John and Almeda's baby, Abraham." Ruth twisted a shirt in her hands even though it didn't need more wringing. "I don't want to work at night either. I already feel like I'm being watched."

"Do you have an idea as to whom? Do you think it's the King Gang? Do you think they are after you or one of the children?"

In late August Sheriff Riverby had warned the ladies to take care because a new outlaw gang was in the area. They were known as the King Gang and attacked when and where they wanted. It was the same gang who had kidnapped Chloe so many years ago, holding her for many years before abandoning her when she was about to give birth to Lil-Pen. Nugget Nate had had one of his Callings. Along with his wife, Penny, he had found Chloe nearly out of food for herself and Duncan, and in labor. After she'd given birth, they'd taken her and the children to Sanctuary Place. Chloe, Duncan and Lil-Pen had lived there until they moved to Stones Creek.

Ruth realized she had panicked her friend. "It's nothing really. More a product of my past. You know my story. That man." She never called her rapist by any other name. "He had been watching me for several months. I was young and oblivious to everything. When he attacked me, he told me he'd been watching me for a long time. Now, I notice. Notice things that aren't even there. I can't not notice. I'm always thinking someone is watching me. Even when there aren't any men around."

Ruth had been raped and left pregnant by a prominent businessman. Her family didn't believe her and kicked her out.

Nate had found her and taken her to Sanctuary Place where she had given birth to her daughter Kathryn who was now eleven.

Laura wrapped an arm around Ruth's shoulders. "Ruth, don't discount your feelings. Woman's intuition, it's real."

Ruth just nodded. She did feel as though she was being watched. Sometimes she felt like more than one set of eyes were on her. It was silly really. Who would be watching her?

Five of the eight ladies who had come to Stones Creek were now married or would be soon. That left three: herself, Laura, and Blanche. None of them had beaus. Well, Laura seemed to have caught the eye of the barber, but he hadn't made any moves to get permission to court her.

None of the women were required to marry, but they needed to find a way to support themselves until they did, or in case they didn't. Since the area was vastly lacking in available females, no one thought there would be a need for long term employment.

"Have you figured out when you have these feelings the most?" Laura asked.

"Well, when I'm on the porch some or in the yard with the children. At least during the summer. Not so much now, but we are inside more with the weather colder. When I'm out on Main Street. At church." Ruth gave a harsh laugh. "Seems it's any time I'm where men might be, or at least where I can be seen by men."

"That's not much help in pinning it down."

"No."

~~~~~

The children of Sanctuary House were running and playing with the rest of the Stones Creek and surrounding ranches' children after worship service on Sunday. There was some shoving going on, too, but not enough yet for the adults to get involved.

It was warm for mid-November and sunny. The adults were chatting about the double wedding that had been held the week before. Two ladies of Sanctuary House had been married. Cora Sepal had married Deputy Dak Levine, and Myra Hope had wed Sheriff Newt Riverby. There were jokes made of the two lawmen getting handcuffed and jailed by the women.

Laura came out of the church after speaking briefly to Pastor Noah Preston. He was one of the four men charged with approving the men who wanted to court the House ladies. Laura was somewhat disappointed that no man had requested permission to court her. She glanced at Hank Johnson who was talking with several other men. He turned his head and looked at her, then he touched his hat and went back to paying attention to Arty Massot, the town's very busy carpenter. He was building houses and furnishings as fast as he could. He was nearly finished with Ben Cutler's residence.

Once they moved in, hopefully sometime in December, Chloe Ashburn and McIlroy, the blacksmith, would be getting married. That would leave only Laura, Ruth Naylor, and Blanche Basking, and their children living in the house. With winter fast approaching, it was doubtful more ladies would be coming from Sanctuary Place in Iowa to join them.

"Ma'am."

Laura turned at the male voice addressing her. "Hello, Mr. Dickerson. How are you this fine day?" Laura smiled up at him. He was about average in height, and she came up to about his chin. Broad shouldered with a stubble beard, he had on a black cowboy hat and gray duster coat under which black boots peeked.

"Mighty fine, Mrs. Duffle. Saw you standing here and thought I'd bring you a bit of news. I believe I mentioned, at the school, raising that Mr. Mader was selling the Bent Arrow Ranch. Well, the sale is complete. It's now Hawk's Wing Ranch, and I've been promoted to foreman."

Laura could tell he was proud of his promotion, as well he should be. He looked to be in his early thirties. "Congratulations, Mr. Dickerson. That's a notable achievement."

"Thank you. I believe you're right."

A slight grin pulled at Laura's lips. Seems Mr. Dickerson had a bit of a pride issue. But then, most men did it seemed to her. The thought sobered her. She was exhibiting some pride herself with her judgmental attitude.

"Mama, are we leaving soon? I'm hungry." Mark pulled on her skirt to get her attention.

"Who's this?" Mr. Dickerson asked. He knelt down, so he was about eye level with Mark.

"I'm Mark, and I'm seven and three quarters. My birthday is in Febury. I'm gonna be eight then."

"Well, eight-years-old, huh. You looking for a job as a cowboy? I just might be hiring in Febury."

Mark looked up at his mother, excitement at the idea sparkling in his eyes. "Can I be a cowboy after I turn eight, Mama?"

"I think you might need to wait just a bit longer than that."

Mark turned back to Mr. Dickerson, disappointment evident on his face. "Mama says I gotta wait. You think I'll be ready when I'm nine?"

"Might be, but we'll defer to your mother on that. Just know, when the time comes, you'll have a job if you want one." He stood and tipped his hat to Laura. "Ma'am, it's been a pleasure chatting with you. Hope we have the chance again real soon." With that, the new foreman of the Hawk's Wing Ranch turned and moseyed over to his horse, untied the reins, and mounting, headed out of town at a canter.

"Well, he certainly singled you out, Laura." Ruth placed a hand on Laura's back as she spoke.

"What do you mean?"

"He came out of the church, walked right up to you, had his conversation, mounted and left town without speaking with anyone else. Pretty pointed declaration I'd say."

Laura barely kept her jaw from dropping open. Red Dickerson interested in her? She'd only spoken with him two other times since she'd moved to town. Then again, he had made a point of talking with her at the school raising. That might not really count as just about every man in a ten-mile radius had spoken with her and the other House ladies. But, if what Ruth said was true, he had made a point to speak with her and tell her about his promotion to foreman. Maybe it was his way of indicating interest in courting her.

Laura tipped her head down and to the side just a smidgen. She could observe Hank without it being noticeable to anyone else. His focus was on the dust settling from the passage of a horse heading out of town.

CHAPTER FIVE

Laura kept busy with laundry for Hank and the other men who wanted her services. Every day she had a batch of towels to wash for the barber and several loads for the single men of the town and surrounding ranches. Those who thought to save a few coins by wearing their clothing far too long to be cleaned with only one wash and rinse found the charge to receive their clothing back was far more than bringing it to her sooner.

Laura was enjoying her job and the freedom of having money she earned herself. She was her own boss and felt secure in her capability of supporting herself and her sons. But it was hard work, and she was tired by the end of the day.

Only a month into her business, she had been able to purchase the laundry tubs needed, freeing up the House's tubs to be used when the ladies wanted to use them. Laura's next goal was to purchase a kettle to place over her fire to heat the water, so the one she used would go back to being only for House activities.

Maybe one day she'd have a place so she could do the washing inside. Then she'd have a stove and a copper boiler. The thought excited her, but ultimately, one of those new-fangled rotary laundry machines with a mechanical ringer was her goal. Laura was going to be saving whatever she could to attain her goals.

Daily, she opened the back door to Hank's shop and took the basket filled with face and bath towels. Most days, face towels far outnumbered the larger ones. Toward the end of the week, and especially on Mondays, the number of bath towels increased with the number of men who came to bathe in Hanks large tubs on Saturday. Laura often shook her head at the grime left on the towels after they wiped supposedly clean bodies.

Doing the towels first allowed her to return them quickly since they didn't need ironing. She would fold them into the basket straight from the line once they were dry and set the basket just inside the door. Hank paid her weekly. He was the only customer who was given his laundry back before she was paid.

Today, Laura was heading around to the front entrance of the barber shop. Vernie Preston, Pastor Noah Preston's wife, was hosting a tea for the ladies of the church on Thursday. Since all the ladies of the House wanted to attend, Laura needed someone to tend her boys after school.

She didn't think the tea would last too much past the dismissal time, but wanted to be sure they were supervised until she could get to them. Duncan Ashburn, Ozzie Basking, and Kathryn Naylor would be watching the House children, but Laura was just a bit unsure that her two would behave. Eddie, especially, was pushing the boundaries set down by his mother and the other adults of the House. Besides, Hank had expressed the desire to get to know her sons a bit more. This seemed a good chance to offer a short time to do just that.

No one was in the barber chair when Laura looked in the window. Hank was facing the counter doing something with his supplies so Laura opened the door and walked in, not something she would do if he'd had a customer.

"Afternoon, Hank." Laura smiled at him. He was handsome she thought. Maybe not the best-looking man ever but pleasing to her. He was always neat, had been even before she began doing his laundry. He had on a white shirt and black pants. Black suspenders ran up his back molding the shirt to his frame. There were black armbands holding his sleeves away from his wrists.

She hoped he would want to court her, but he hadn't made any indications that he was interested. Maybe he was afraid of taking on a family. That was another thing she hoped to accomplish with him watching her boys, getting Eddie and Mark acquainted with Hank a bit more.

Turning around, Hank smiled a greeting. "Afternoon, Laura. What brings you into the shop?"

Laura twisted her fingers into the fabric of her skirt. "I was hoping you would do me a favor."

"Anything."

Laura laughed. "You really don't want to offer that. You don't know what I might ask for."

"No, I suppose I don't. Okay, how about—if it's in my power, of course." Hank finished wiping a comb and laid it on a towel on the counter.

"Mrs. Preston is having a lady's tea at the church on Thursday afternoon. All the ladies of the House are planning on attending. I, um, well—It will most likely go a bit longer than school. Several of the older children will be watching the younger ones, but I was wondering if you would be willing to have Eddie and Mark here for the time?

"You had stated you wanted to get to know them better. I'll make sure they know that what you tell them needs to be obeyed. I think they would enjoy watching you work. They've never been to a real barber. We just do the clipping needed at the House." Laura's words tumbled from her mouth at a rapid pace.

Hank picked up a razor and his strop, stroking the blade along the leather. "I don't see that as a problem. Might not have any customers even. Often don't on a Thursday. It would give me a chance to get to know them a bit. How long do you think I'd have them?"

"I can't think more than an hour. Mrs. Preston must know most of the women have children who will be dismissed from school mid-afternoon."

Hank smiled at her. "I'd be most pleased to host your boys for an hour or so on Thursday." He winked at her. "Just put the fear of God in them about minding what I say. I was a boy at one time myself, you know."

~~~~~

A plate of cookies sat on a high shelf beside the mirror above the counter waiting for the Duffle boys to arrive. Hank had gone to the bakery next door and purchased a variety to offer them, remembering how hungry he had always been when he'd gotten home from school. Maybe they would get a snack at the House before they came to stay with him at the barbershop, but he wanted to be ready to feed them if they came straight there.

One thing was concerning him, however. He'd been unusually busy this afternoon. A number of men had got off the morning westbound train and entered the hotel earlier in the day. Several had come into the shop requesting shaves and baths. Employees of a railroad company, they were having a meeting in Stones Creek to decide if a spur heading south would be built here. More arrived on a later train. Now, he had one man in the chair, two more wanting shaves, one in each of the bathing rooms, with all the rest of the men in the shop also wanting baths. Hank would be busy tending to not just the barbering, but also the bathing needs.

Hank knew Laura would understand if he canceled, but he didn't want to disappoint her. He also wanted to spend time with her boys, but this crowd in his shop wasn't going to allow that.

He wiped the last of the shaving soap from the customer's face and raised the back of the chair. "You're all done here. Have a seat, and as soon as there's a bathing room available, you'll have it."

The man stood and moved to a chair, expressing his thanks. Hank went down the hall and knocked on each of the two doors, calling that the bath time was up and they should finish and dress. He pulled his pocket watch from his vest and marked the time. If they weren't out in around five minutes, he'd knock again.

He asked the next man to get in the chair as he heard running footsteps on the boardwalk outside. He was wrapping the man's face in a steaming towel as the door opened and two boys entered, stopping dead in their tracks as they saw the five men looking at them.

"Come on in, boys," Hank said, making sure he gave a smile of welcome. "It's a bit crowded at the moment, but it'll clear out some shortly. I've got some cookies here if you're hungry."

The tentative looks on the young faces vanished, and they came forward, pulling their caps from their heads as they came. Hank noted that both boys could use a trim and hoped he'd have time to give them one before their mother came to get them.

He settled the boys in a corner with the plate between

them and went to tend the bathing rooms, getting them prepared for the next bathers. The men were chatting with the boys about their favorite subjects; lunchtime and recess, when he came back.

"Eddie," Hank said. "Can you get towels and place two in each of the bathing rooms, for me, please?"

"Sure," the boy's excitement over having a job was palpable. "From the basket Mama brings back?"

"Yes."

Eddie ran down the hall while Hank began shaving his customer.

"Their mother is at a church tea and asked if I'd watch them after school."

"She does Mr. Johnson's laundry. A bunch of other men's clothes, too," Mark said around the cookie he'd stuffed in his mouth.

"Oh?" one of the railroad men said.

"Yes, she has a laundry business here in town. Much appreciated by the single men around these parts." Hank tipped his customer's chin a little.

"Hear tell you have single women here in town," another man said.

Hank went on to explain about Sanctuary House and the women and children living there. Meanwhile, the men who had bathed, paid and left. Eddie came back and sat beside his brother, scarfing several cookies off the plate. With wide eyes, he also watched Hank as he shaved, then trimmed the hair of the man in the chair. That made Hank stand a little taller. Having the youngster interested in his work appealed to him.

It wasn't long before all the waiting men were shaved, and the last two were being led down the hallway to the bathing rooms. Once they were settled, he'd spend some time talking with Eddie and Mark. He hoped they'd ask him questions about barbering since he didn't really know what else to talk with them about.

When he reentered the shop, he stopped, took in a breath to yell, then, instead, leaped forward, grabbing the straight razor from Eddie's hand. Hank couldn't speak. His heart was pounding, and no air seemed to be in his lungs.

Little seven-year-old Mark was swathed in the large white and blue striped apron. Shaving soap was daubed on his face and neck. He looked so little sitting in the big chair. A thin line of red stained the foam on his throat.

"What did you think you were doing?" Hank finally gasped out. He looked from the slowly welling blood to Eddie.

"I was gonna shave Mark." Eddie looked at his brother, and his eyes rounded wide. "I cut him. I cut his throat. Is he gonna die? Did I kill him?"

Mark put a hand to his throat. "Ouch. The soap stings."

Hank threw the razor onto the counter and, grabbing a towel, wiped the soap away from the cut. Relief flooded him. It was a slight wound. No more than a paper cut on a finger. It could have been a tragedy though.

Eddie was crying, and Mark was holding his fingers over the cut which wasn't really bleeding anymore. Hank gathered both boys in his arms and mumbled what he hoped would be comforting words. He was totally lost with what to do.

The shop door opened, and Laura walked in.

~~~~~

Laura smiled as she pushed the barbershop door opened. She'd had such a good time at the tea. Leah Steele, Norie Pierce, Almeda Wilson and Sara Cutler were becoming good friends to all the ladies of the House. So was Vernie Preston, but she really had to be since she was the pastor's wife.

Laura wished she'd had a new dress to wear, but her one good dress had to do. Everyone had seen it before. Most of the women only had one good dress which they wore every Sunday and to any event worthy of their best outfits.

Several of the town women weren't interested in becoming friends, exhibiting disapproval of the House ladies. They were the ones who, from the first proposal of Sanctuary House, objected to ladies of questionable background moving to Stones Creek. Though they didn't speak their disapproval at the tea, the sentiment was evident.

Even with the frowning ladies, Laura enjoyed the tea. They had made plans for the children's Christmas pageant and planned a potluck for New Year's Day, weather permitting.

As Laura stepped into the barbershop, her smile froze on her face. Hank stood there with a boy on each arm. Eddie was crying and Mark, wrapped in a barber apron, had spots of shaving foam all over his face. She drew her eyebrows together. Something was wrong with his hair.

"Um, what's going on? Is everything okay?"

Eddie began crying harder. Mark wiped a hand across his face, got some of the soap in his eyes, and began crying. Hank looked like a rabbit smelling a fox. If he hadn't been holding her sons, he would have been running out the back door as fast as he could.

Laura picked her younger son out of Hank's arms and set him on the counter, moving the razor to a high shelf. Placing a towel in the basin, she poured water on it and proceeded to wipe the soap from his face. Once Mark was cleared of foam and had stopped crying, she shifted her gaze to Hank. Eddie had stopped crying too, so the shop was quiet.

"Okay, what did these hoodlums do?"

"You're mighty calm for coming in on that scene," Hank

said.

"As the mother of two boys who live in a house with five others, not much other than copious amounts of blood or bones sticking through skin upsets me."

"Mama, I'm sorry. I didn't know I coulda killed him."

Laura shifted her gaze back and forth between Mark, Eddie, and Hank. "Well, now I might get upset. Tell me what happened." Laura knew her voice was tight, and she really needed to know just what she had walked in on.

"I've been really busy this afternoon. Some railroad men came to town today and wanted shaves and baths. There are still two in the back rooms now. The boys had been really good." Laura saw Hank flick his gaze between them. "I left them with a plate of cookies to tend the bathing rooms and came back to—"Hank swallowed, his Adam's apple lifting as he did so.

Laura lifted an eyebrow.

"Eddie was attempting to shave Mark." Hank swallowed again, then hurried on. "I grabbed the razor, but there was a tiny cut. It stopped bleeding almost immediately. I think it was more of a scrape than a cut."

She turned back and examined Mark's throat, relieved when she found the small red line. It was as Hank described. Not more than a shallow scrape.

Laura stabbed her older son with a stern glare. "Were you supposed to touch any of Mr. Johnson's barbering equipment?"

"No, ma'am." The words were uttered barely above a whisper.

"What did I say the consequences would be if you touched them?"

"No dessert for a week and, um, have to stay in my room

after school every day for a week."

"So, where are you going right at this moment?"

Eddie lifted his face from looking at the floor to peer at her. "To my room."

"That's right and no dawdling. Now git. No, wait. Do you have anything you should say to Mr. Johnson?" Laura drew her brows together and tilted her head. Eddie got the message.

"I'm sorry, Mr. Johnson. I shouldn't have touched your things."

Hank cleared his throat. "No, you shouldn't but— You've learned a lesson, I hope. If you don't know what you are doing, barbering tools can be dangerous."

"Yes, sir." Eddie turned to leave then turned back. "Sorry, Mark. I didn't mean to hurt you."

"It didn't hurt much. The soap in my eyes hurt worse."

Laura cleared her throat. Eddie headed down the hall and shortly, they heard the back door open and close.

"I'm sorry, Laura," Hank began.

She held up her hand stopping him. "Mark, honey." Laura turned to face her younger son. "Why did you let Eddie try to shave you and um…" She flicked her fingers through his hair. There were chunks missing from various places all over his head. Seems the boys had been left to themselves a bit too long.

"You said I needed a haircut and Eddie had been watching Mr. Johnson cut the men's hair. He said he could do it since it looked so easy."

Laura pulled her lips between her teeth to keep from laughing or even smiling at Mark's assessment of what it took to be a barber. She glanced at Hank. His mouth was pulled down in a frown. No doubt about it. Her sons hadn't endeared themselves to him.

Just then voices could be heard approaching from the hallway leading to the bathing rooms. It must be the railroad bigwigs. They entered the shop, and Hank spent a few minutes chatting and being paid. Once they left, he came to her side with tentative steps.

"How about I fix the mess Eddie made of Mark's hair?" The question was asked quietly.

"I'd appreciate that. I'm able to do a simple trim but this —" Laura flicked Mark's hair again. "It's beyond my skill level. Even though my children seem to think barbering is a pretty easy thing to do." She eyed Mark letting him know his opinion was in error. He looked down and fiddled with the apron he was still enveloped in.

Hank grabbed a wide board from beside the counter and placed it on the barber chair. It straddled the arms, raising the seating area. Sitting Mark on it, he picked up a comb and pair of scissors. Laura stepped back.

Spying the empty plate on the floor, she stooped and picked it up. "Just how many cookies were on here to begin with?"

~~~~~

Hank swept the last of the hair on the floor into the dustpan and dumped it into the wastebasket. Laura simply amazed him. She had seemed so calm and collected during the entire unfortunate episode. She was picking up around the shop while he cleaned up the mess Eddie had made of Mark's hair.

Since Laura hadn't wanted him to shave the boy's head, there were still places that were shorter than others, but time would take care of that. Hank had told her to bring him back in a couple of weeks, and he'd trim it more evenly. Right now, his scalp would show through in a few places.

Hank picked up the board he'd thrown onto the seat of the barber chair when he began sweeping. When the back door closed behind Mark as he headed back to the House, Laura had shoved it off, letting it slam onto the floor with a loud bang. She'd flopped down in the chair and curled over placing her face in her hands.

"Oh. My. Word. I can't believe Eddie thought he could not only cut Mark's hair but also give him a shave with a straight razor. What was he thinking?"

Then she'd looked up at him. Her eyes finally revealing the stress of holding her emotions in while her sons had been in the shop.

"It's my fault. I should have made sure the boys understood they weren't to touch the tools." Hank's guilt at what might have happened ate at his soul. Laura had trusted him with her most precious possession, her children, and one might have been grievously injured.

"Yes, you could have told them, but they had been warned by me, and they chose not to obey. The responsibility for their obedience belongs to them. There is no temptation we don't have a way out from, if we will take it. I don't know how many times I've told those boys that. But I'm just their mother. And they are just boys."

Hank watched her shoulders slump in defeat. He realized then that it must be extremely tough to raise boys without a father in the picture. His father had been the one to place the fear of God in him. To show him that there was always someone to be accountable to.

Boys needed men to be that for them. They knew they would grow up and be physically stronger than their mothers. There would come a time when character mattered more than strength of body. That making the right choice came from an inner strength rather than an outer one. Some men never learned that.

"Laura, I'm sorry. I know I failed you and them. I…"

"No, Hank. You know boys." She grinned at him. "You were one once. I'm sure you got into just as much trouble as mine did today. Thankfully, nothing but a bad haircut and small scrape on the neck were the consequences. At least we didn't need Doc Eli. That's always a blessing."

Even though Laura was smiling at him, Hank still felt the weight of the events of the last hour.

CHAPTER SIX

Hank opened the door to the barbershop and stepped outside. "Come on in, Eddie. It's cold out here. I don't want you to catch a fever." The next day was Thanksgiving, so he'd been busy all day. It was late afternoon, and school had let out at noon. There would be no school on the holiday or the day after.

The nine-year-old turned red from being caught spying in the window. With shuffling steps, Eddie passed Hank and entered the warmth of the building.

"So, what are you doing, standing outside looking at me?" Hank crossed his arms over his chest. He wasn't angry at the lad. No, he was pleased the boy seemed interested in him.

"I like watching you cut hair and shave the men. You do it real good."

That pleased Hank even more. Eddie was impressed with his skills. Hank thought about McIlroy taking on Chloe Ashburn's son Dunc and teaching him blacksmithing. McIlroy was certainly enjoying it. But then, Dunc was thirteen, nearly fourteen now. That was old enough to begin learning a trade. Eddie was only nine, not near an age to begin training. Still, spending time with the lad would help Hank learn more about Laura. It couldn't hurt him to get to know the boy.

"Would you like to watch me more often? Maybe even earn a few coins?" Nothing wrong with sweetening the offer a bit. Besides, there were small chores Eddie was probably capable of doing.

Eyes, very much like his mother's, lit with excitement. "Yeah, how?" Eddie bounced once on his toes.

"Well, let me see. How about sweeping up the hair on the floor after I'm done with a customer? And restocking the towels in here and maybe in the bathing rooms. Those are both very important jobs. Sometimes I get mighty busy and don't have time to do them properly. When you're here, you could do those. I'd pay you a penny a day." Hank remembered the stipulation McIlroy put on Dunc. "But, only if you keep your grades and chores up. If I hear you're letting either slip, your time here will be over."

Eddie nodded, then sobered. "Do I gotta come every day?"

"No, if you have something you want to do, like go and play with Seth Cutler or do something else, that's just fine. The days you want to be here and do the work, I'll pay you. If you don't come, you won't get paid. If you want to come and just watch but not do the chores, you won't get paid. That's okay, too."

Eddie thought about it. "Sounds fair to me. How about we shake on it?"

Hank's lips twitched as he fought the chuckle wanting to escape. Eddie's countenance was so very serious. He held out his hand. "Okay, we'll shake to make the deal." When Eddie reached to take his hand, Hank pulled his back. "On the condition that your mother agrees."

Eddie pulled his lips sideways. "Oh, all right. I suppose she has to for this to work. Shake."

Hank and Eddie shook hands. "Come on." Hank grabbed

Eddie up and tucked him under his arm by the waist. "Your ma will most likely be out back. Let's go find her and seal the deal."

Hank had Eddie turn the knob to open the door leading to the alley and backyard of Sanctuary House. Laura was there taking laundry off the lines. Hank hadn't put on a coat, and the cold air chilled him quickly. He pulled his eyebrows together with concern.

"Mrs. Duffle," Hank began. When she turned, he continued. "This here young 'un's been spying on me. I have caught him red-handed."

"Oh, Mr. Johnson. I'm so sorry. It won't happen again." She quickly came forward reaching for Eddie. Laura's distress nearly had Hank quit his teasing.

"No, you can't have him." Hank stepped back, turning slightly, so Eddie was more behind him. "I've decided to keep him. At least for a while. We also brokered a deal betwixt us." Hank was pleased to see she caught on to his game.

"Oh, just what kind of deal? How long do you propose to keep Eddie?"

"I think until supper time tonight. Then whenever he wants to come and watch me barber. He's taken the job I've offered him. All it needs is your approval."

"A job, you say. Just what sort of job is this?" Laura was leaning back eyeing him with teasing suspicion, her arms crossed in front of her, some piece of laundry hanging from her fingers.

"He's to sweep the hair on the floor and restock towels in the shop and bathing rooms. I'll pay him a penny every day he comes and works."

"My Eddie, you'll be rich before you know it." Laura ruffled Eddie's hair as he hung against Hank's side.

"Yeah, and I don't have to go every day. Just when I want to. I only get paid when I go, but that's fair."

"Only if you do the work while you're there," Hank reminded him.

Eddie had lost interest in the conversation. He'd garnered his mother's approval, and now more important matters came to the forefront of his mind. "I'm hungry. Can I go get a snack?"

Laura smiled. "Only if Mr. Johnson is willing to release you. He said he had you until supper time."

Eddie's head snapped around so he could look up at Hank. "Can I go get a snack, please? I haven't eaten in a really long time. I'll come right back when I'm done. I promise."

"Sure, Eddie. I wouldn't want you fainting from hunger while you work." Hank set the boy on his feet.

As he ran toward the house, Laura called, "Do whatever your afternoon chore is for today if you can. That way you'll have it done and won't have to worry about being home in time to get it completed before supper."

"Yes, ma'am," Eddie called as he ran up the back porch steps.

~~~~~

Hank watched the boy disappear into the house. That had gone well. Laura seemed to appreciate his taking an interest in Eddie. He turned his attention back to her.

Watching her fold whatever article was in her hands made him aware again of the cold chill of the wind slipping between the buildings. Laura was wearing a coat and bonnet. He wondered how she worked in the wash water in the cold.

Focusing on her hands, Hank noted that they were red and looked chapped. He thought of the months to come. Winter wasn't even here yet. It was over five months until warm weather returned.

"Laura, how are you going to do laundry during the winter? Are you going to be working outside?" Hank was afraid he knew the answer.

"Most of the time. There isn't room in the House for me to set up inside along with the work that needs to be done there. I can't use the stove to heat the water when the cooking needs to be done."

"You can't be working out in the cold. It's not healthy." Hank took hold of one of her hands. "Look at how chafed your hand is, and it being only November."

"It'll be fine, Hank. I'm used to it, or getting there."

"No, it's not. Look, I have a room in the back of my shop that I don't use. Well, I do, but just for storage. There's a stove in it. I had planned on making it into a third bathing room but haven't been busy enough to need it as such. I'll rent it so you can work inside. I'll make the modifications needed for lines and put in a bench for your tubs. I'll even help carry water if I'm not busy."

"Oh, Hank, you don't need to do that. I can work out here."

"No, Laura. I insist. You'll catch your death of pneumonia; then where will your boys be?"

Hank watched as tears filled Laura's eyes.

"Okay, thank you. I wasn't looking forward to the cold and working in the water out in the weather. How much do you want for rent?"

"I'm willing for you to do my laundry for free. That'll be enough for me."

"Oh, no. That's not nearly enough." Laura started to protest more, but he placed his fingers on her lips.

"No arguments. You can keep doing my laundry for free in

the summer when you are back out here in the alley." He watched her eyes begin to twinkle.

"So, you're going to kick me out come warm weather, huh?"

"Well, it'll get mighty hot in there in the summer. But you can work inside then if you want."

"Maybe only on rainy days. I have trouble working when it rains."

"It's settled then. I'll go and see what needs done to make the room fit for your work. I think I have a bench up in my apartment that might work, at least until we can come up with something permanent."

Hank turned to head back into his building. A small reddened hand placed on his arm stopped him.

"Thank you, Hank. I truly appreciate it."

Looking down into her face, Hank felt his heart swell at her gratitude. Maybe he'd more seriously consider speaking with Pastor Preston and the rest of the men entrusted with the futures of the Sanctuary House women.

~~~~~

As Laura and Ruth were doing the supper dishes, they talked about Hank's offer.

"He was quite insistent I use his backroom. Said he didn't want me to take sick. Asked me what the boys would do if something happened to me. I'd not thought about that. It's what made me accept his offer.

"Ruth, if something ever happened to me, you'd take my boys and raise them, wouldn't you? Please?"

Ruth put her arms around Laura. "Only if you promise to do the same for my Kathryn."

"Of course." Laura hugged her friend, best friend really. "You suppose we ought to get some sort of legal document about it? Not that there's a lawyer anywhere closer than Denver." Laura giggled a bit.

"Heard tell that Sheriff Riverby's contacting one and having him draw up adoption papers for Troy. Oh, did I tell you I'm going to have him to watch again? Myra is going to go back to working for Leah Steele in the dress shop. Myra wants to continue at least part-time now that she's settled after the wedding and all. You know, Leah's nearly ready to birth the baby and wants Myra to help even more once the baby's born."

"That's wonderful for you. Did I see you talking with Massot the other day after church?"

"Yes, seems he heard I might be looking to take on some cleaning jobs. He's asked me to come on Saturday and look at his place. He lives in a couple of rooms above his carpenter shop." Ruth laughed as she placed several plates she had dried on a shelf. "He said the place was a disaster, and he hadn't a clue as to how to fix it. Thought it might need a woman's touch."

"And you're that woman?" Laura lifted her eyebrows and smiled.

"At least to clean the place up. Massot wants me to work on Saturdays, so I won't have to work there at night. Ben said I could dust shelves on Saturdays, too. Sara's not going to be as available to help once they move into their house."

"Will that be enough to earn you what you need?" Laura handed her another washed plate to dry.

"Well, maybe. If I could get a couple more small jobs, it would be better, but I don't really see how to fit them in. We'll see." Ruth's uncertainty about her work situation showed on her face.

Laura wiped her hands on a towel and drew her friend close for a hug. "The Lord will work it all out for you. Keep praying for the solution. I will, too. I know He'll supply all your needs. It says so in His Word."

"You're right. I just have to stand on that promise."

"Let's get this done. I know the other ladies are wanting to get started on preparing for Thanksgiving dinner tomorrow." Laura released Ruth, and they went back to doing the dishes as fast as they could.

CHAPTER SEVEN

Red Dickerson walked into Noah Preston's gun shop. As much as Red liked and respected the preacher, he had a hard time reconciling the man's two professions. He'd never heard of a minister who was also a gunsmith. Red had heard the tale of Noah's childhood trauma. He'd watched his mother and sister be assaulted, and his sister kidnapped as Noah's father stood by doing nothing to stop the attacks. Red supposed that would affect how a man saw the world and his place in it.

"Morning, Red. How goes things on Hawk's Wing?" Noah wiped his hands on a rag and reached one across the counter to be shaken.

"They go well. Hawk finally arrived and seems to know most of what he's doing. Handles a horse mighty fine, he does. Not afraid to ask questions, either. He could probably stand to come and avail himself of Hank's services. His hair reaches halfway down his back. Keeps it tied back with a thong."

"So you're satisfied to work for him?"

"Yeah, not looking to move on anytime soon. Actually Preacher, I'm looking to see if you and the other men will approve me to do some courting. Now that I'm foreman, I've got a house and enough of a wage to support a wife and family."

"I see. How about we head over to Ben's? You go see if Doc Eli's available, and I'll check at the jail for Sheriff Riverby." Noah took his black duster from a hook on the wall and slipped his arms into it. Next, the black Stetson went onto his head. "Let's go. Meet you at Ben's in a few minutes."

The four men met on the boardwalk in front of Cutler's General Store, greeting each other before they entered. Soon, Red was drinking coffee with the others and Ben around a table in the back room.

"So, you're looking to join the rest of us in wedded bliss, huh, Red?" Sheriff Riverby asked.

"Hopin' I might."

"Be careful who you pick. I've got me a real spitfire. Myra might not be the best at housekeeping, but even her standards are higher than mine. She's shaped me up pretty fast."

The other men all laughed at the tall sheriff. He and Myra had shot sparks at each other before they began courting. Now, Newt was in contact with a lawyer in Denver about adopting her five-year-old son, Troy.

"A wife will certainly change your life." This time it was Doc Eli Steele speaking. "First, the woman brings adjustments, then come the babies." Eli was grinning from ear to ear. His wife, Leah, was expecting their first child sometime around Christmas.

"Both are blessings from God," Noah said.

"Most of the time," quipped Ben, who had been married the longest and was a father to three children. All the men laughed. That Ben loved his wife and family and was devoted to them was evident to all in Stones Creek.

"So, Red, you're thinking of courting one of the House ladies?" Noah turned the topic from general to specific.

"Thought I might see if you'd approve me doing so."

"I've no objections. Do any of you men?" Noah looked at each man of the committee.

They all expressed their approval. Red was pleased none had reservations.

"Which lady are you considering?" Ben asked.

"I'm thinking to court Laura Duffle. I've been making a point to speak with her most Sundays. She seems pleasant, and I know she's hardworking. I have her do my laundry. Actually dropped it off before I came to speak with you, Pastor."

"You willing to take on her sons as your responsibility?" Eli asked.

"Yes, I understand they come with her. Mark's a cute scamp. He asks me questions about my horse every time I see him. Don't know Eddie quite as well, yet."

"We men." Newt indicated the others of the group. "We've decided that any man who wants to marry one of the ladies with children needs to be willing to adopt the children. You thinking along those lines?"

Red thought about that. It hadn't occurred to him that adopting the boys would be required of him. "I understand your concern for the children. Laura's situation isn't the same as some of the other ladies. She's a widow. She may not want to have the boys adopted and change their last names. I'd be willing if she wants to. That would be her choice, not mine."

Noah clapped Red on the shoulder. "Mighty fine answer there, Red. Should be her choice. They are her children. You'll need to take on the role of the father with all that goes along with it."

"I know, Pastor. I'm planning on it."

"Good to hear." Noah looked at the other men. "We good here, or do you have any other questions or thoughts?"

"Nope, I think we're good," Ben spoke for the rest of the

group.

"Can I ask a question?" Red said.

"Think you just did." Newt quipped.

"What would you have said to me if you hadn't approved?"

There was a chuckle from each man. Noah answered, "You'd have never gotten this far. We've talked, at length, about the men we think would make acceptable husbands to the ladies. Any men we don't want courting them are refused, as gently as possible, by whichever of us they approach to inquire. Seems it's always me, though."

Everyone laughed at the disgruntled look on the preacher's face.

"And a better man there isn't for that task." Ben slapped Noah on the shoulder.

~~~~~

Hank heard the front door open, causing the attached bell to jingle. He was cleaning out a bathing room after the man had left.

"Hey, Hank, you here?"

The voice was that of Hank's friend, Red. He was always glad to see him. "Coming," he called. Hank placed the towels in the basket outside the door to the room where Laura now did her laundry. She'd been working there for a couple of weeks, and Hank was enjoying having her in there. He could chat with her between customers, and most of the men were coming through his shop to drop off and pick up their laundry. Red had done so just that morning. Hank wondered what had brought his friend back so soon. His laundry wasn't due to be picked up until Saturday.

"What brings you here again?" Hank asked as he entered the barbershop room.

"Need a shave and a haircut." Red hung his coat and hat

on the hook on the wall by the door and sat in the barber chair. "I just got permission to do me some courtin'."

Hank's stomach did a funny tightening. Something told him he wouldn't like to hear who Red wanted to court. "Oh? Who are you planning on courting?"

"Thought I'd be asking Mrs. Duffle if she'd be willing to take some walkabouts with me. She's a pretty little filly, and the boy, Mark, seems partial to me. Haven't really had much doings with Eddie yet. Seems he's always with some friends while I'm chatting with his ma and brother."

Yep, that's what Hank was afraid of. He'd waited too long to decide to ask the men if he could court one of the women. His indecision had him losing the woman he was interested in.

That hesitation in making decisions had cost Hank several times in his life. But he'd been burned by making choices too quickly too. Seems he never could find the right balance.

As Red went on chatting while his hair was being cut, Hank took note that he wasn't really talking about what attracted him to Laura. It was more that Red was looking forward to having a woman in his life. Hank didn't get the impression that Red was specifically describing Laura. That bothered him. Laura was pretty special. At least Hank thought so.

Red was one of Hank's best friends though. Hank and Red went way back. They'd worked on the same ranch when Hank had tried out being a cowboy. Red was one of the reasons Hank had settled in Stones Creek when he'd finished his barber training. Red was working on the Bent Arrow Ranch then, the same one he was now the foreman of, though the owner and name had changed.

Hank was glad when he could wrap the hot wet towel around Red's face, softening the stubble, and stopping the chatter.

As he stropped the blade, he reconciled himself to be happy for Red and Laura. Red would make her a good husband. He was hardworking, faithful, and constant. He'd raise the boys to be fine men. Hank pushed aside the thought that it was what he, himself, had wanted to do.

As he put the payment for the shave and haircut into his moneybag, Hank said, "Well, good luck with your courting. Hope it pans out for you." Inside, he was thinking the opposite. He didn't want the relationship to work out. He wanted Red to fail. If he did, Hank would be right in there to pick up any broken pieces he left behind.

~~~~~

Laura was setting the table for supper when a knock came at the House front door. Since she was the only one there, she answered it. Red Dickerson stood holding his hat in his hands.

"Afternoon, ma'am. Might I have a moment of your time?"

Laura noted that he'd been shaved and trimmed since she'd seen him earlier that afternoon.

"Um, no one else is here right now. Let me get my coat, and we can sit on the porch." Laura did so, and soon they were seated on the swing in the corner.

"Mrs. Duffle, um, I was wondering if, um, if I could come courtin'? I got permission from Pastor and the other men. They are agreeable if you are."

Laura was surprised, but then also not. Red made a point every Sunday after service to speak with her. Mark often showed up, and Red gave him some attention which her son looked forward to.

Hank's face flashed through Laura's mind. She liked Hank. Really liked him, but he hadn't made any moves to try to court her. Red had. And courting wasn't marriage. It was just seeing if they would suit.

As much as she was enjoying working for herself and being able to support her family, Laura longed for the security of marriage, as well as the closeness with another person. Okay, she admitted to herself. She missed being with a man. Laura and her husband had been close and in a very loving relationship. She missed him and the physical aspects of her marriage.

"I think that would be agreeable. We can court, and you can get to know the boys and me better, as we can you. How often do you plan to come to town? It must be hard in the winter to make the journey."

"Unless the weather prevents it, I should be able to come a couple of times a week as well as Sundays for worship service. Shall we set up specific days?"

"I think that might be best. I can adjust my work on those days, so I've time to devote to you. I can also make sure the boys are here much of the time. Plan on joining us here at the house for Sunday dinner, also. All the suitors do. It'll just be Blanche Basking, Ruth Naylor and myself here after Chloe and McIlroy get married a week from Saturday."

"I'd be pleased to join you."

Once they'd decided on Wednesdays and Sundays as the days he'd come courting, Red stood.

"I'll be taking my leave now. I've got things to do on the ranch. Hawk's here now, and we meet most days in the late afternoon and talk over the day. I'm going to be late today, but I had business here in town to tend to." Red smiled at her. "I look forward to seeing you again, Laura. I hope it's okay for me to call you by your first name."

Laura felt herself blush. "Yes, of course, Red. One question though. You have dark hair. Why do they call you Red?"

"It's 'cause of my first name. It's Reddington, named after my mother's maiden name. Too much of a mouthful to say, especially when someone's hollering it acrost a herd of cattle."

Laura giggled a bit. "I can understand that."

~~~~~

As Red rode back to the ranch, he thought about his afternoon in Stones Creek. He'd accomplished much. He'd dropped off his laundry, gotten permission to go courting, as well as a shave and haircut, and spoken with Laura Duffle who was willing to see if they'd suit.

She was attractive, if a bit plump. Red figured having two children might do that to a woman. He didn't mind. He did like her dark hair. It looked long, though it was always piled up on her head. Looked soft, too. He'd like to see it down and run his fingers through it.

Red had been wanting a woman in his life for a long time. Now that he was foreman on Hawk's Wing Ranch he could afford one. Laura Duffle met his requirements. She was hardworking, a believer, and pretty. Yes, she'd do.

CHAPTER EIGHT

Laura and her sons waited for Red to arrive to take them to the wedding. Chloe Ashburn was marrying McIlroy, the town blacksmith. No one knew his first name. He simply went by McIlroy.

Mark was bouncing, eager for Red to arrive. He liked the idea of possibly moving to the ranch.

Eddie was sullen. He was not excited about the prospect of the cowboy courting his mother. He didn't want to think it might be possible that they would leave town and move onto a ranch if Mr. Dickerson and his mother got married. Even the lure of having his own horse wasn't enough to encourage acceptance of the idea.

Laura had warned Eddie that he had to be polite and take the time get to know Mr. Dickerson. There was a possibility that he'd become their step-father. That comment had caused her oldest son to start crying. He wanted Mr. Johnson to be his step-father, not a cowboy.

Taking Eddie up to her bedroom, Laura sat with him on the bed. She'd seen Chloe arrange herself, Dunc and Lil-Pen, her children, against the headboard to talk about serious issues.

"Eddie, I understand that you like Mr. Johnson. He's a

good friend of mine, too. But, Mr. Dickerson has asked to court me, us. Mr. Johnson hasn't."

"Maybe he will if I ask him."

"No, Eddie. You can't do that. If he wanted to come courting, he would have. He's had plenty of time to decide whether he was interested. Mr. Dickerson is interested. He went to Pastor Preston, Doc Eli, Mr. Cutler and Sheriff Riverby and asked them if he could court me. I'm going to honor his request. We'll get to know him and see if we suit. If we do, and Mr. Dickerson asks, I may decide to marry him. If that happens, he'll be your pa."

"But, I want…"

Laura placed her fingers on Eddie's lips stopping his words.

"I know. But Mr. Johnson hasn't made any moves to show he wants to court me or become your pa. Mr. Dickerson has."

The bones seemed to go out of her son. Instead of remaining beside her, he collapsed onto her lap. He cried out his disappointment that the man he was looking up to didn't seem to want him.

Laura held him as he cried. She felt the same way. Although she liked Red well enough, it was truly only as a friend. The man she was attracted to was Hank Johnson. At times, she thought he might reciprocate her feelings. He was so very kind to her. Helping her to develop her laundry business. Letting her rent his backroom to wash in during the winter. Carrying water for her when he had time. He'd made the advertising sign and strung lines up in her washing room so she could hang laundry out of the weather.

But he had never mentioned courting her nor had he gone to the group of men to request permission. Red had, and that's why she was willing to be courted.

Laura didn't want to be alone. She was managing to make a living and raise her sons by herself. It was hard work. The ladies of the House helped and supported each other, but the burden of guiding her children to adulthood was totally on her shoulders. They needed a man's influence. Needed that male role model, so they learned how to be honorable, God-fearing men. That was something she couldn't give them.

So, as much as her heart might long for Hank Johnson, it was Red Dickerson who very well might become her husband.

~~~~~

Hank stood at the back of the church. He didn't need to sit. The small building was filled with the residents of Stones Creek and the surrounding ranches. McIlroy had done blacksmithing for nearly everyone and was friendly and helpful, in general, so he was well liked. Besides, when the vows were spoken his full name would finally be revealed. Everyone wanted to know what it was. He'd never told, only saying he was McIlroy, just McIlroy.

Hank beat his hat against his leg. Laura and her boys were seated next to Red Dickerson. Hank was kicking himself for not having taken the initiative to speak with Pastor Preston and the others. It was a failing in his character Hank was going to work to change. His indecision had cost him for the last time. Though he, sort of, hoped for the best for Laura and Red, in his heart he knew he wanted the relationship to fail. If it did, he'd be over at the gun shop asking Pastor if he could court Laura faster than a mule could kick.

Hank realized he hadn't been paying attention to the ceremony when the congregation burst out laughing. From his position, he couldn't see the couple very well, but he heard Chloe's voice.

"I don't care what your name is. I love you anyway."

Rats, he'd missed McIlroy's name.

~~~~~

Red hitched his horse to the rail in front of Sanctuary House. A wagon was parked in the yard with the two draw horses also tied there. It must be Harvey Hayes' wagon. Red knew he'd married Birdie Pullman from the House back in September. Stones Creek's Sheriff Riverby and Deputy Levine also had married House ladies. They'd be here to celebrate Christmas too.

Red opened his saddle bag and took out the parcel with his gifts for Laura and the boys. He hoped they liked what he was giving them. Mark seemed to accept him. Eddie was still reserved. Maybe the gifts would help.

His knock was quickly answered by some child he didn't know. The boy stepped back to let him in.

"Merry Christmas. You here to be with Mrs. Laura? I'm Ozzie Basking."

"Merry Christmas to you, too, Ozzie. I'm Red Dickerson, and yes, I'm here for Mrs. Laura and Eddie and Mark, too."

Mark came running and wrapped his arms around Red's legs. He looked up and smiled at Red. "Merry Christmas. We're gonna eat dinner soon, then open presents, and then go to church. We got turkey an' stuffing an' punkin pie an' apple pie an' mince meat pie."

"You going to eat all those kinds of pies?" He grinned at the excited little boy swinging back and forth as he hung onto Red's leg.

"Not mince meat. Yuck."

Laura appeared in the doorway to the dining room. "Welcome and Merry Christmas. Come on in here. It's much warmer."

Red followed her and saw that nearly all the original ladies, as well as their husbands, were there. He knew one had married a trapper and left town. He'd watched all the ladies since their arrival in Stones Creek and tried to figure a way he could support one. When Hawk bought the ranch and made Red foreman, the opportunity arose.

A couple he'd considered too young for him. They were both married now. Blanche Basking was older than him and had four children, so he'd ruled her out. He didn't mind the thought of taking on children, but four seemed too many.

That had left Chloe Ashburn, Laura Duffle, and Ruth Naylor. All were the right age and only had one or two children. McIlroy had set his sights on Mrs. Ashburn, so he'd been down to two. Although Mrs. Naylor only had one child, it was a girl, and he didn't know much about girls. Also, her job was minding the children while the other women worked. Even though he figured Ruth knew all about running a home, Laura's skills at laundry tipped the scales in her favor.

The large dining room with its many tables and chairs was decorated for the holiday. There were paper chain garlands hanging between the sconces on the walls. Each table had a centerpiece of pine boughs and cones tied together with red ribbon atop the white tablecloths. Laura had told him they didn't use those tablecloths normally. They were kept for Sunday dinner and special occasions. Well, Christmas was a special occasion.

The aroma from the pine boughs mixed with smells of turkey and all the trimmings welcomed Red. Mark was still attached to his leg.

"Here, Cowboy, take this parcel to where the presents are." Red handed it to Mark who released his leg and ran off. He greeted the other men, and they chatted amiably while the ladies bustled around getting the feast ready to serve.

As soon as all was ready and everyone seated, Blanche Basking stood.

"Thank you all for joining us today. It would have been a lonely day without our House ladies who have wed celebrating with us. Now, let us say grace and enjoy the bounty of our Lord."

Once everyone bowed their heads, Blanche began, "Our gracious and Heavenly Father, we come to you today with thanks and love. Without the birth of your Son, Jesus, He could not have grown in wisdom and understanding to live a perfect life, preached Your new covenant, taken all our sins on Himself to die on the cross. Without His death, He could not have risen to prove His power, might and triumph over death and the evil one.

"So, we come humbly to You, asking Your blessing on the meal provided by Your loving work. May we honor You with our lives in all we do. In Your precious son, Jesus' name, Amen."

Before she even sat down, dishes were being passed, and food was spooned onto plates.

Red sat next to Laura, with Mark between them. Eddie sat across from him with a frown on his face. Knowing the boy preferred Hank over himself irked Red. He also knew he needed to give Eddie time and attention in order to win him over. Maybe the gift he'd brought would help with that.

Myra and Sheriff Newt Riverby sat at the table with them, her son, Troy sitting at the end. Myra was a spitfire who kept them laughing with her rather earthy comments about the quirks of the customers who frequented the dress shop, run by Mrs. Leah Steele, where she worked. Even though Myra didn't say the names, everyone knew or suspected about whom she was speaking.

"Well, Mrs. Leah finally succumbed and padded the bodice. When the customer comed to try it on, I 'most died. I wanted to burst out laughin' but managed to hold it in. Just as we'd been tellin' her for months, it hung cockeyed and sagged. All that paddin' outside of the corset just cain't not sag. Mrs. Fu..." Myra bit off the name.

"The missus stood there looking at herself in the full-length mirror. She looked so sad." Myra's tone had changed from jovial to concern. "Finally she said, 'Mrs. Steele. I do believe you were right. Is there anything you can do to fix this?' Mrs. Leah placed a gentle hand on her back an' told her that, of course, we could. When we was leavin' so the missus could change, I done heard her mumble, 'now how am I going to get his attention?' Made me feel right sorry for the missus. All she's a wantin' is a bit of her husband's notice." Myra took a bite of turkey.

Newt placed an arm around his tiny wife's shoulders. "I don't have that problem. If I don't pay you any mind, I get an earful and then some." Myra's head snapped around, and her eyes flashed sparks. He leaned down and kissed her nose. "And I'd never ignore you anyway. I love you too much to ignore you. Besides, you're way too much fun to tease."

Everyone at the table, as well as the ones nearby whose occupants had been listening, began laughing. Myra smacked Newt on the arm, but she was smiling as she did so.

Once dessert was enjoyed and the tables cleared, the presents were distributed. Each family had opened their gifts as a unit before everyone arrived for the meal. The children all had one gift to open from the Ladies. None could afford to give to each person, so it was decided that a knitted hat was something every child would benefit from during the cold winter. Yarns in a variety of colors had been purchased with pooled money so the child's favorite color could be use for their gift.

When Eddie brought his bag to their table, Red wondered for a moment if he should have brought something for everyone, then decided it was a foolish thought. He'd never have been able to afford it, and he hadn't even known how many there would be.

After opening his pack, Red handed a gift to each boy and Laura. "Now, boys," he said. "These are for both of you, so you'll have to share. You each get to open one, but they are equally both of yours."

The boys nodded before tearing the paper off. In Mark's was two whittled horses. Not being a very good whittler, Red had bought them from one of the cowboys on the ranch. The delight in Mark's eyes, and his quickly uttered thank you, told of his pleasure of the gift. Troy, who'd come to stand behind Mark was handed one horse, and the boys began galloping them around the room, as Mark climbed down from his chair.

Eddie watched for a moment then, glancing at his mother, said, "Thank you, Mr. Dickerson." Then, he turned his attention to the gift in front of him. A joyous cry of, "Jackstraws," indicated the acceptance of the game. "Thank you." Eddie jumped up and ran to where several of the other boys were gathered. Upon seeing the new toy, the boys claimed a table, now empty, and spilled the sticks to begin playing.

"You made progress with him today," Laura said. "Those were thoughtful gifts. And I appreciate you cautioning them that the toys were joint for them both. It will save a lot of arguing."

"Hey, I was a boy once myself and have several brothers. We might not have had many toys, but were quickly made to know that no one of us could claim ownership."

Laura started to rise, but Red placed a hand on her arm. "I got you something too. After seeing all the hats, I'm not sure you'll be pleased with it." He pulled another bundle from the bag, giving it to her.

"You didn't need to get me anything. Now I feel awkward. I didn't get anything for you."

Red could tell the lack of a gift bothered her. He grinned and tapped her on the chin. "You can do my laundry for free this week. That's a good and practical gift." His suggestion brought a small smile to her face.

"All right. I will." Laura's focus turned from Red to her gift. She pulled the paper off and chuckled. "I can see why you'd think I might not be welcoming this, but it's lovely." She ran her hands over the skeins of yarn. "Oh my, it's so soft."

"I thought the color would look good on you. Mrs. Cutler said there's enough for a knitted or crocheted shawl. Not too sure what the difference between them is, but I figured you'd know."

Laura laughed. "No, I don't suppose you do."

"Children," Ruth called. "Put your things up. You need to get over to the school to get ready for the Christmas Pageant. We'll come back here after service so you can play and visit again before everyone goes home."

All the school-aged children abandoned their toys to get coats and mittens. The new hats graced all the heads as they burst through the front door yelling Merry Christmas as they went.

~~~~~

Laura excused herself and headed to the kitchen. The dishes needed to be done before they left for church. She found herself with a towel in her hands, drying.

As she wiped a plate, Laura thought about the gifts Red had given. She still felt badly about not thinking to purchase anything for him, but she truly didn't have enough money to spend on luxuries. Eddie had needed new pants as he'd suddenly sprouted two inches taller. All the hems had been let down as much as was possible. Mark had fallen and torn the knee out of one of his pairs. That it was a hand-me-down worn by Eddie and several other of the House boys made the loss less important, but she'd had to purchase a pair of trousers anyway.

Those and gifts for the boys had eaten into her ready cash. Laura hadn't considered delving into her savings to buy a gift for Red. The thought that he might purchase her something hadn't crossed her mind. His idea of doing a week's laundry for free at least gave her a way to honor his gift to her.

Laura set the dry plate onto the shelf and turned back to receive another one. The kitchen was crowded since everyone wanted the job done quickly. Some of the ladies were beginning preparations for the evening meal. Others were doing clean up from this one.

"It was sweet of Mr. Dickerson to bring you a gift, wasn't it?" The questioner was Chloe McIlroy. She was just back from three days in Denver with her new husband. They'd picked out furniture for the apartment they were living in above Cutler's General Store.

"Yes, it was."

"You don't seem enthused."

Laura chuckled. "Even Red realized the gift might seem more like work after seeing all the hats we made to give the children."

"Are you alright? You seem, I don't know, pensive."

"I'm fine. I know I can't expect Red to be like Alan. I know

I need to be grateful he wants to court me and that he gave me a gift for Christmas. It's just…" Laura paused. "I didn't really expect to receive anything. Now I feel guilty on two counts. One, I didn't get him anything. Two, I wish his gift to me had been a bit more, I don't know, personal."

"Are you sure you are making the right decision to be courted by him?"

Laura placed another plate on the shelf. "He's a good man. He's a believer. He's steady and a hard worker. He brought gifts for my boys."

"Those are all good, but they don't answer my question." Chloe placed a hand on Laura's arm keeping her from moving to get another dish.

Laura looked at Chloe. "He's the one who asked me. No one else has been interested enough to ask to court me."

~~~~~

The men of the Stones Creek area were dismayed when they heard a man had been hired as the schoolteacher. Just what we need, they thought, another single man around here. That had changed when Mr. Hiram Bergdorf arrived in early September. He was in his early fifties and a widower.

Hailing from Chicago, he had a son living in Wyoming and a daughter in Denver. Both were married with families. Mr. Bergdorf didn't want to impose on either of them, so he took the job in Stones Creek.

Mr. Bergdorf was well liked by his students and their parents. When he'd approached Pastor Preston about having the children put on a pageant telling the Christmas story at the worship service on the holiday; Noah had decided it would be a good way for the children to learn about the birth of the Savior. After they ended the play, Pastor Preston would preach about the connection of the birth to the cross. Mr. Bergdorf thought the idea delightful. Noah thought the word unusual for a man to use. But, they parted pleased with the plans.

The students had been practicing for over a month. All the speaking parts were memorized, and those without parts had been tasked with tending the animals who would be participating in the pageant.

Costumes were gathered and stored at the church the week before the event. Most were clothing from the children's parents. The angels wore men's white dress shirts, their sleeves rolled up. Stiff white paper had been purchased for the children to make wings. Twine looped around the arms of the angels at the shoulders held them in place. Some were a bit lopsided, but the pride of the creators made them beautiful. Mrs. Steele had donated yellow ribbon for halos. She'd even stitched the lengths into circles.

The shepherds were dressed mostly in brown work shirts. Their headdresses were flour sack towels tied on with twine.

Mary had on a blue dressing gown. The sleeves were wide and wouldn't stay rolled. She kept flipping her hands to keep the cuffs out of the way. A navy blue shawl was wrapped around her head, covering her blonde hair. Joseph looked similar to the shepherds, but his shirt was green. He also had a sash torn from an old sheet.

The three wise men were disgruntled that they had to wear women's dressing gowns. They were more colorful and looked much richer than any man's garment. Allowing the boys to make crowns out of the yellow paper and then glue bits of colored papers cut from canned goods labels eased the discomfort somewhat. Each of their gifts was a box or small chest borrowed from their mothers with warnings that it better come back in one piece, or they would find themselves in just as many pieces.

Rather than risk a live infant, Mr. Bergdorf had borrowed a baby doll to represent the Christ child. It was swaddled in a baby blanket which was tied on with twine so it wouldn't come unwrapped while the production was going on. A shipping crate filled with straw stood as the manger.

The included animals were a donkey, a yearling steer, several sheep, and a pony with padding on its back covered with a blanket to represent a camel. Because of the number of children and animals in the production, the pews had been moved back a bit to allow the extra space needed.

Now, the children were gathered in the school next to the church, in costume and waiting for Mrs. Preston to come to let them know everyone was seated and the first hymn was being sung. Mr. Bergdorf had made sure everyone had used the outhouse before putting on their costumes.

Mrs. Preston opened the door, and all the chatter that had been filling the room ceased.

"I think I'm going to be sick," a young girl's voice said.

"Don't be dumb. You're just an angel. You only gotta sing. No one's even gonna to know you're there." It was a boy's voice in response.

"Quiet now, children." Mr. Bergdorf clapped his hands. "Let's go. Stay in your proper line, please. No talking. We'll do this just as we did in rehearsal."

They all tramped outside. The boys in charge of each animal untied the leads from the hitching rail and tugged them to the church. Two boys leading the steer and donkey went up the aisle and tied them to the legs of a chair, then headed down the aisle to the back.

Mary and Joseph, played by Kathryn Naylor and Duncan Ashburn, went up the center aisle. Mary laid the baby in the manger.

"It is just as the angel said," Duncan said loudly. "You, Mary, have given birth to a baby boy."

"Yes, Joseph." Kathryn's words were spoken much more quietly. "We shall call him Jesus, Emmanuel, God with us."

"He fulfills the prophecy in Micah.

'But you, O Bethlehem Eph'rathah,
 who are little to be among the clans of Judah,
from you shall come forth for me
 one who is to be ruler in Israel,
whose origin is from of old,
 from ancient days.'"

They sat down beside the shipping crate manger.

The angels and shepherds, towing their sheep along with them, came up the aisle and to the side of the platform. It took several minutes to get everyone arranged with the youngest, shortest angels and shepherds in the front. Then the tallest angel, Ozzie Basking, stepped forward. The shepherds shrieked in fear causing the sheep to begin bleating.

"Do not be afraid," Ozzie hollered. *"I bring you good news of great joy that shall be to all people. For unto you is born this day, in the city of David a Savior, who is Christ the Lord. And this will be a sign for you: you will find a babe wrapped in swaddling clothes and lying in a manger."*

Then the multitude of angels behind him began singing the familiar words, "Glory to God in the highest, and on Earth peace among men with whom he is pleased!"

That everyone sang them at a different speed, which made the words nearly unintelligible, didn't make any difference to the congregation. The speakers were their children and friend's children.

Ozzie led the angels down the aisle to the back of the church.

"Let us go over to Bethlehem and see this thing that has happened, which the Lord has made known to us," Eddie said after being poked by another shepherd. The herd of shepherds and sheep moseyed across the stage and gathered behind Mary and Joseph.

Seth Cutler, Junior Brook, and Will Basking marched up to the stage in their colorful dressing gowns. Junior was in charge of the 'camel.' That the animal didn't want any part of the play was evident in his stiff legged gait and bobbing head. He whinnied and snorted his displeasure. Will's crown fell off, stopping the procession until he was able to rescue it before it was stomped by a hoof.

When they arrived on stage, the sheep recommenced bleating because of the commotion of the 'camel' trying to find a way out. Finally, Junior pulled the animal as far away from the sheep as he could, turning him, so the pony faced the corner. That seemed to calm the beast.

"We have come to worship the King of the Jews 'cause we have seen His star in the East," Seth said.

Junior yelled his line from his spot in the corner. "We followed it for many days, for we are wise men from a distant land."

"And we brung gifts for the child; gold, frankincense, and myrrh."

Just then Mary jumped up and screamed, "EEWWW." She snatched the baby doll from the shipping crate and ran up the aisle. "That cow just pooped," she said as she went.

The noise of liquid hitting the floor sounded. The other children on the stage began scattering as the stench of manure and urine began filling the church. Mr. Bergdorf and Pastor Preston hurried through the fleeing shepherds, sheep and wise men. The donkey, not enjoying the sudden smells, noise, and movement, began braying and jerking his head. He began stamping his hooves.

Junior had managed to pull the camel-pony up the side aisle, leaving only the steer, donkey, Mr. Bergdorf, and Pastor Preston at the front of the church. The teacher grabbed the rope tied to the steer and, pulling it free, tugged the beast into motion. He carefully sidestepped the pile and the liquid running across the floor.

Pastor Preston attempted to calm the donkey but wasn't having much luck. The animal began kicking and brayed even more loudly. Tied to the chair, it was unable to move very much, but its movements turned it until the hooves came in contact with the shipping crate, breaking it into pieces that went flying toward the first row of pews. The men sitting there jumped, shielding the women and small children.

Pastor Preston, finally managing to get the rope untied from the chair, stepped in the pile left behind by the steer. Winding the rope around his arm, he tightened it until he'd pulled the donkey's head down, forcing the animal to stop kicking. He stood there for several minutes to allow the donkey calm down before leading him quietly up the aisle and out the door.

With all the animals tied outside, Mr. Bergdorf came over to Pastor Preston. He cleared his throat and said, "Well, that certainly was not delightful after all."

~~~~~

The occupants of the House had just finished breakfast when the back door opened, and then slammed shut. Everyone looked at the door to the kitchen. Myra Riverby flew into the room.

"I just had to come and tell you. Leah Steele's done give birth to a healthy baby boy. They named him Steven after her pa. She had it last night 'bout one-thirty. Doc Eli come an' asked me to open the dress shop today." Myra's eyes danced with excitement.

Chatter about the blessed event filled the room. The boys were less enamored than the ladies and girls. Discussion centered on when to visit and deliver the various gifts the ladies had made.

Laura stood, picking up her plate and flatware. "I need to get to work. I've got a lot of laundry to be doing." It was true, but not the reason she wanted to get across the alley and into the barber-bathhouse building. "You boys obey Ruth today." She ruffled Mark's hair and rubbed Eddie's back just a moment before she went into the kitchen and set her dishes on the counter.

She entered the back door to Hank's shop and carried the bucket of water she'd pumped into the kettle on the stove. There was already a fire going so Hank must have been down earlier.

Laura had had to move the straw they insulated the pump with to keep it from freezing. Once she had hauled all the water she needed and had containers for, she would put the straw back and wrap the blanket around the stack, securing it with a rope. Laura wished the pump was in the building, but it serviced every business and apartment in that building, as well as the House.

The room was simple with only the stove, a low table for the wash tubs, an ironing board, one straight chair, and the strings of clothesline suspended from the ceiling. Hank had supplied the line and hooks, as well as hung them. He'd also installed three shelves next to the stove. On them, she kept her irons, bars of soap, starch, and whatever else she needed or brought with her.

It was Monday, so she had several bags of laundry cowboys had brought on Saturday. Cowboys tended to come on Saturday since they got paid on Friday. Some came Friday, but usually after she was finished for the day. Then, they went to the saloon.

If they were still in town Saturday morning, they'd drop it off then. Some just left their bags in the alley near the door. They would come the following week to pick it up and pay her. No one got their laundry back until the money was in her hand. She'd learned that the hard way.

Hank wasn't around, so he must have started her fire then gone back upstairs to his apartment. Monday wasn't a busy day for him. She couldn't wait to tell him about Leah's baby.

That thought stopped her in her tracks. Shouldn't she be wanting to share the news with Red? Well, she did, but Hank was in town, and Red wasn't. Yes that was it. She wanted to tell Hank simply because she couldn't tell Red.

CHAPTER NINE

The New Year arrived, along with a telegram brought to Sanctuary House by Ira Bragg the stationmaster/telegrapher. He was smiling as he handed the yellow paper to Blanche, striking a pose meant to show off his physique. She pressed her lips together hoping it looked like a smile. The young man was conceited, thinking he was much more attractive than he truly was. He also couldn't figure out why none of the young ladies living in the House wanted to chat with him very much.

Since she didn't have any coins, she offered a few cookies, instead, as a tip for the delivery. He stepped further into the foyer as if he wanted to enter the dining room. Blanche called for Nancy to bring the cookies, and, when she did, gave them to him, ushering him back out the front door. She didn't like the way the telegraph operator/station master looked at her daughter.

Going into the parlor where Ruth and Laura were busy wiping down the walls, Blanche opened the folded paper. "Hum, seems as though we will be getting some new residents."

The others stopped working and looked at her as she read the telegram out loud.

"Greetings stop

"Glad to hear of marriages stop

"Sending Gema Volkovichna and Libby Trembly stop

"Arriving fifth stop

"No children stop

"Betty Sanctuary Place"

"Who's Libby Trembly?" Laura asked.

"I don't know. She wasn't there when we were. I'm surprised Betty is sending her out here when she can't have been at the Place very long." Ruth went back to wiping down the walls.

Blanche folded the note and tucked it into her apron pocket. She would pass the news on to the other women who were already married when she saw them next. They would all want to be there to meet the train when Gema and Libby arrived.

~~~~~

On Thursday, the westbound train was late arriving. It was late afternoon, and a cold wind was blowing so the ladies huddled next to the station trying to stay warm. Each one understood the insecurity of arriving in a new town not knowing anyone, so they wanted to meet the train.

Gema Volkovichna, they all knew. She was an orphan who had come to Sanctuary Place when her parents and siblings had died of influenza as they migrated across the country after immigrating from Russia. She hadn't known any English at the time and still struggled with the language. Sometimes she still mixed up or left out words, leading to confusion or laughter. She had turned twenty just before the original Sanctuary House ladies left Iowa.

Libby Trembly was an unknown, but they were going to welcome her with open arms. Each lady at the House had experienced rejection and condemnation and wouldn't inflict that upon anyone.

A train whistle sounded in the distance. Ira Bragg stepped out of the station and pulled out his pocket watch.

"Twenty-five minutes late," he said and moved to stand near where the baggage car would stop. Laura hid a grin and exchanged a glance with Blanche. Again, the young man stood as if he had a tail like a peacock to show off.

"Struts like a cock, don't he?" Myra's softly spoken comment nearly made Chloe sputter.

"Hey, don't make me laugh. Who knows? Maybe Gema or this Libby will think he's just wonderful."

"Doubt it." Myra murmured, reaching to grab Troy by the collar before he could stray too far from her skirts.

The noise of the locomotive made conversation impossible until it had passed the station and stopped, leaving the passenger and baggage car next to the platform.

"Myra, Cora, Ruth, Chloe, Blanche, Laura." The call of names came from the train car, and all the ladies looked up and saw the beautiful blonde waving, obviously eager to descend the step the conductor was placing. As soon as he lifted his hand to help her down, she jumped, bypassing the step altogether. She ran across, arms wide and wrapped them around as many of the ladies as she could.

"I had missed you muchly. I am so pleased have arrived. Where are Esther and Birdie?" She chattered as she hugged each of the six ladies who had come to meet the newest residents of Sanctuary House. "Oh, please to make acquaintance to Libby. You have met her not. Come."

"Gema, slow down," Blanche hugged the excited young woman.

Gema laughed. "Yes, I must. So excited am I." She took a deep breath and drew out of Blanche's arms. "Come."

The other woman was standing timidly near the train. Laura was startled by the deep sadness in her eyes. Something very tragic had occurred in her life.

"Libby, these ladies are those I explain about." Gema began making introductions when she was interrupted by the stationmaster who had helped the train crew unload two trunks and a large wooden crate.

"Mrs. Basking, is this all the baggage? The train needs to get on its way."

Blanche looked at the newcomers.

"Yes," Libby said.

"Will you see they are delivered to the House, please, Mr. Bragg?"

"Of course, ma'am. It'll be my distinct pleasure." His gazed raked up and down Gema's figure.

Myra, her back to the man, rolled her eyes.

Laura leaned close to her friend and said, "Just keep your mouth shut. Sometimes you let words out before you start thinking."

Just then Newt and Noah rounded the station building. Myra's expression broke into a huge smile. Newt came to her and kissed her on the top of her head. Gema's eyes got wide.

"Gema," Myra said, taking Newt's hand and pulling him over to meet her. "This be my husband, Sheriff Newt Riverby. He's gonna adopt my Troy. Where is that boy anyway?" She looked around. She found him squatting down, looking at the wheels of the passenger car.

She called him to come back. When he looked up and saw Newt, he jumped up and ran to him. "Pa. Pick me up."

All the ladies exchanged smiles and pleased glances.

~~~~~

Once they had Gema and Libby settled in their rooms, the

ladies gathered in the parlor where they had placed the large wooden crate that had been delivered to the House along with the trunks. Ozzie Basking had taken a crowbar and pried off the lid.

"These are for all brides. We all made them for you." Libby pulled out a beautifully embroidered pillowcase. Chloe was stunned, as were Myra and Cora. The crate was full.

"Each bride, for herself, will take sheets of full set and twin for all child unless they sleeping double will be in big bed. Then, one for it. Also, set of dish towels, seven, for each day of week one. All they are embroidered," Gema said. "Everyone helped with stitching. Some are... more exacting than others."

"There are more than enough for all who came in July," Libby added the last.

"How're you gonna get them to Miss Esther?" Eleven-year-old Kathryn Naylor asked.

That question led to explaining her sudden marriage to the trapper, as well as Birdie's marriage to Harvey Hayes.

Several of the ladies left needing to complete supper preparations. The others unpacked the crate, sorting the items into patterns on the sheets and pillowcases and days of the week for the dishtowels. Myra, Cora, and Chloe were first to choose the designs they liked. Birdie would be allowed her choice when she next came to town, most likely on Sunday, if the weather held. Then, the rest would be saved until the next wedding.

CHAPTER TEN

By the end of the following week, both Libby and Gema had found work. Libby was hired as a clerk at Cutler's store. Mrs. Cutler, Sara, was expecting her fourth child and having a difficult time. Ben didn't want her having to tend the children, their new house, and the store when she was feeling so poorly.

Gema found work as a maid at the hotel. It worked well since her command of the English language, while good, didn't lend itself to having to speak and be understood.

Red rode into town and saw the slim blonde crossing the road. She wasn't someone he'd seen before. Sitting atop his horse, he watched as she walked beside the café toward Sanctuary House. Turning Ralph, his horse, Red headed to follow her. He wasn't interested, of course; he had a different purpose for coming to town today. But she was new and sure pretty.

"Mr. Dickerson." Mark's call pulled his focus to the boy running across the yard. "Whatcha doing here today? It's not Wednesday or Sunday." Those were the days of the week Red came to do his courting. He also picked up his clean laundry and dropped off the dirty on Wednesdays. Today was Saturday, and Red let the hands come to town and spend their earnings.

It was a warm January day, rare in these parts, so several of the children were outside playing.

"Well, buckaroo, I just thought I'd come and surprise you, your brother, and ma. Thought I'd take you all to lunch at the cafe. What do you think of that?" Red dismounted and tied Ralph to the hitching post.

"Hurray. I've only eaten there once. I'll go get Eddie. He's at the barbershop."

"Where's your ma?"

"Doing laundry. Want me to go get her, too?"

Red ruffled Mark's hair. "How about we go together since they are both in the same place?" It sort of stuck in Red's craw that Eddie spent so much time with Hank. Well, that could change real soon.

Red and Mark went around the House and up the alley to the back entrance of the barbershop. Opening the door, Red let Mark precede him into the hallway. The boy ran ahead to the front. Seems that was where Eddie liked to spend time.

Red turned into the nearest door and found Laura up to her elbows in sudsy water. "Howdy."

Laura looked up and blew at a tendril of hair that had escaped the pins. "Hi, what are you doing in town today?"

Red chuckled. "Same thing Mark asked me. I came to take you and the boys to the café for lunch."

"Oh, well." Laura looked from Red to her tub and back to Red. "I suppose I can leave this. Um, let me..." Laura lifted her hands from the wash water and grabbed a towel, proceeding to wipe them dry. "I'll need to go to the House and fix myself up a bit. I'm not fit to be in public like this."

"You look fine to me." Red scanned up and down her body. He liked her figure well enough. She was a bit thick around the middle but had decent curves. The image of the tall, slim blonde flitted through his mind.

"Well, I need to clean up anyway. My hair is falling all around me." Laura's hands fluttered around her head. Then, she ran them down the front of her apron. Red noticed it was damp and soiled.

"All right. Mark went in to get Eddie. How's about I go get the boys, and we'll meet you in the parlor at the House when you're ready?"

"That's good. I won't be long." Laura set the stove to conserve the fire and, grabbing her shawl, stepped past him and out the door.

Red headed up to the front room, finding Mark, Eddie, and Hank. "Hey, Hank."

"Hey, Red. What brings you to town today?"

Again! Red chuckled. "I must be pretty predictable. That's the third time I've been asked, and I've only spoken to three people. Hi, Eddie." Red reached out and patted Eddie's shoulder.

Eddie looked at Red and turned away.

"Eddie." Hank's voice was firm. "You be polite. We've talked about this."

Eddie turned back. "Hello, Mr. Dickerson. Glad to see you."

Red could tell he wasn't. "I came to take you and Mark and your mother to the café for lunch. How does that sound?" He saw a spark of interest in Eddie's eyes. "She went to freshen up a bit before we head over there. We're to meet her at the House, in the parlor. That'll give you two a chance to wash up. Well, I suppose I could use some, too. I'm dusty from the ride."

Eddie looked up at Hank, then shifted his gaze to Red. "Okay, let's go. Come on, Mark."

The boys ran down the hall. The back door slammed open then closed, leaving Red and Hank looking at each other.

"Your courting going well?" Hank asked, turning to straighten his scissors, razors, and combs.

"Seems to be. Hoping it goes even better. I'm thinking of making the relationship permanent."

Hanks' hands stilled, and he laid them on the counter. "Well, let me know when congratulations are in order."

Red was concerned about his friend. He didn't seem his normal, contented self. There seemed to be a pall over him and the shop. Red had expected that his friend would be happy for him. It didn't seem he was.

Had Hank been interested in Laura? If so, why hadn't he said something when Red first mentioned his thoughts of courting her? He'd have stepped aside. It wasn't as if he loved Laura. They didn't know each other well enough for that to have developed.

Oh, well. There wasn't anything he would do about it now. Hank had had his chance and not done anything with it. It was Red's turn. He just hoped it didn't end their friendship.

~~~~~

Laura watched Eddie carefully. He wasn't exactly impolite, but he was skirting the line, giving one-word answers to the questions Red was asking. Mark was eating up the attention he was being given.

They were seated at a table near the window in the cafe. Having ordered, they were now waiting for their food. This wasn't something the boys were familiar with. At Sanctuary Place and House, the children weren't called to the table until the meal was ready to serve.

"How much longer, Ma?" Eddie asked.

"It won't be too long. They need to fix our meals. They'll bring you a plate of food."

Eddie slumped in his chair.

"Tell me about catching the pig that ran away again." Mark looked up at Red with eager anticipation.

As he retold the tale Mark had heard each time Red came to court her since the event had happened, Laura's attention wandered. Was what she was doing, allowing Red to court her, the right thing for her, Eddie, and Mark? She was tired. Six days a week for close to ten hours a day she was elbow deep in laundry. The business had grown beyond what she'd ever imagined. Maybe she should hire Ruth to help her.

But, if Red should decide they would suit she'd be getting married and moving to Hawk's Wing Ranch. Then her business would end. The thought both disappointed and elated her.

As much as she loved being successful and independent, her schedule was wearying. Her back hurt and her hands were chapped. Every evening she coated her hands with a mixture of beeswax, rose water, and lanolin. Then she'd put on cotton gloves to wear as she slept. Even so, her skin cracked and sometimes even bled. It was worse in the winter.

Their food arrived, making the boys extremely happy. And quiet as they ate. Red talked of the ranch and moved on to describe the house he had as foreman.

Laura laid her fork down. She wasn't hungry anymore. It was coming, she knew. Red was going to ask her to marry him. She should be joyously anticipating the question. She had been with Alan. But they'd been so much in love.

The prospect of marrying again was attractive. Laura would have a husband and security. A house of her own. A father for her boys. So why wasn't she excited about the prospect of marrying Red? The image of Hank flashed through her mind. She shoved it away. He hadn't come courting, Red had.

Laura picked up her fork again. She smiled and fluttered her eyelashes at the handsome man sitting across the table from her.

~~~~~

"Do you have time to take a walk with me, Laura?"

They had finished their meal and enjoyed dessert. Red had taken the boys into the bakery part of the café and allowed them to choose several cookies apiece. Now, they were walking up the sidewalk to Sanctuary House. Mark and Eddie had run ahead, wanting to get back to their friends.

"Yes, I suppose so. I do have laundry to get back to, though, so it can't be too long."

"We can just take a short walk. It's so seldom that we get time that's for the just the two of us."

"Yes, you're right. Let me go make sure someone knows to keep watch over the boys."

When Laura returned from her errand, Red took hold of her hand. They walked across the street, passed Massot's carpentry shop, and on to the next street. There were a few houses, including the Cutler's new two story white house with blue shutters. As soon as the ground thawed and foundations could be dug, Massot would start on the house for Eli Steele. The list of houses the taciturn builder had to construct was long. With the advent of the Sanctuary House ladies and subsequent marriages, he'd be busy for quite a while. That row of houses ended the town. More land was plotted out for growth.

Trees grew thicker as they walked away from the settlement. The forest surrounded them with its silence. The scent of pine subtle in the winter air.

Neither spoke until Laura asked, "Whose house is that?" She pointed at a building nestled in the trees. It was unusual. Rather than the standard two or three storied clapboard home, this one was made of logs but was unlike any log cabin either Red or Laura had ever seen.

It seemed a part of the forest rather than having the site cleared of trees to build the house. The first floor was smaller than the upper story which was supported by trees growing through the wide balcony. A six-sided turret graced one corner. Another seemed to have a room built out from the main structure. The eaves extended from the roof over the balcony in several places, providing shade.

As they walked around the building, it became obvious that it wasn't finished. The shell was complete, but markings on the logs seemed to indicate where windows would be cut out.

"I'd say it can only be Massot's. He's the only one I know who could have built such a thing," Red said.

"But when does he work on it? Why doesn't anyone know about it?"

"Maybe they do. This must have taken him a long time to have constructed it to this point. You know how busy he's been building houses and businesses in town." Red looked up at what must be a partial third floor. "As to why no one either knows or talks about it... Well, you've met Massot. Is he someone you'd want to make much conversation with?"

Laura laughed. "No, I don't suppose I would. He's so growly."

This time Red laughed. "Yes, that raspy voice can also put people off."

"It's his attitude that's off-putting. Women think his voice is attractive, stimulating."

Red stepped, so he was facing Laura. He took both of her hands and held them against his chest. "Laura, we've been courting for over a month. I know it may not seem like long, but I think we'd suit well. That we could build a life together. I've got a good job, a house. I can support you, Mark, and Eddie, and any other children that come along.

"I may not have that stimulating voice, but is mine enough to get you to say yes? Will you marry me?"

When Red began speaking, Laura's hands, and her insides began shaking. When he finally asked his questions, she nearly collapsed in a heap, her legs were so shaky.

Laura looked into his eyes, searching for something. She didn't know what. Maybe it was a look that said he truly wanted her. Was attracted to her. Wanted to know her. Wanted to protect and support her.

Red pulled her against his chest and wrapped his arms around her. "Please, Laura. Say you'll marry me."

"Y...yes, I'll marry you." The words came out before Laura could stop them. He was the only man in the area who had expressed any interest in her. Laura knew she wasn't the prettiest of the ladies. Her boys fought some, even in public. They needed a man's influence. Not the occasional mentoring by Hank or some other male who took a temporary interest. They needed a father. Red was offering that. And she was taking hold of that offer.

Slipping his fingers under her chin, Red lifted her face to look at him. Then he lowered his lips, and they met hers. They were warm and pleasant, but the kiss didn't transport her into the throws of desire. He broke the kiss, then placed three more soft, gentle kisses on her lips.

"Thank you. I'm glad we've settled that." Red stepped

back, keeping hold of one hand. "Come, you said you had laundry to do. I won't keep you from it any longer. We can talk about our plans tomorrow after worship service."

Laura allowed him to direct her back through the trees to town. As she walked, she began cataloging the things she needed to do before they got married. First, and most difficult, was telling the boys. Mark would be elated. Eddie... well, Laura just hoped he'd accept the coming change in their lives.

~~~~~

Laura took Mark and Eddie upstairs after supper. She needed to tell them of her betrothal before Red came to church tomorrow. After they washed and changed into pajamas. Laura sat them beside her on her bed. She swallowed. This probably wasn't going to end well for one of her sons.

"You boys remember when we talked before about Mr. Dickerson coming to court me?" When they both nodded, she continued. "Well, one of the reasons he came to town today was to talk more about it."

"No," Eddie said.

Laura patted his leg. "We decided that we would suit and so..."

"NO!" Eddie yelled. "I don't want you to marry him. I want you to marry Mr. Johnson." Tears were streaming down his face. Mark was looking between his brother and mother, confusion and distress on his face.

"Eddie, we talked of this before. Mr. Johnson hasn't expressed a desire to court me." Laura's insides tightened as she said the words. She hurt that Hank was just a kind man, a good man, a man Laura wanted to have been interested in her. But he wasn't. "Mr. Dickerson and I are planning to be married, and we'll all move to Hawk's Wing Ranch. He's foreman and has his own house there. I'm sure he'll give you horses to ride. And there'll be cowboys to teach you to ride and rope and shoot." Laura knew she was trying to entice him with things all boys were interested in, but Eddie didn't seem to care. He lay prostrate on her bed, sobbing.

Mark began patting his brother's back. "It'll be okay. You'll see."

Eddie swung his arm around, smacking Mark on the side. "Leave me alone."

Mark, stung by his brother's rejection of his comfort, began to cry. Laura gathered him in her arms, hugged him close, and rocked back and forth as a tear slipped down her own cheek.

CHAPTER ELEVEN

Sunday morning, Laura, Mark, and Eddie were all tired. She'd let the boys sleep part of the night with her, but their tossing and kicking finally had her moving them to their own beds. She hadn't slept any better, but at least she didn't worry about disturbing them.

They went through their morning duties mechanically. Laura thought back to the morning after Alan had proposed. She'd shared the news with her family and friends at church; the smile on her face stretched so wide it hurt her cheeks. Such a contrast to this morning. She hadn't told anyone, and neither had the boys.

Mark had asked her why Eddie didn't like Mr. Dickerson. Mark thought he would like living on a ranch. He'd miss his friends in town, but having a horse just might make up for that.

Laura had struggled to find words. She knew why. She felt the same. He wasn't the man she wanted to marry, just like he wasn't the man Eddie wanted as a father. But he was the one who asked her.

"I think he'll miss living in town more than you. He's not as interested in ranches and horses. I think that may be part of it."

"Oh." Mark had turned away, maybe not satisfied with her

answer but accepting it.

When they went upstairs to prepare for church, Laura drew them into her room and shut the door. "Now, we are going to be happy when we see Mr. Dickerson. We are going to say we are glad he is going to become your father, aren't we?"

The eyes Eddie looked at her with were filled with despair. "Yes, ma'am."

Laura took him in her arms and hugged him to her. "It's going to be fine. You'll find new interests and lots of things to do on the ranch. Plus, you'll still be coming to school here in town. You'll see all your friends, and we can have them come out to play at the ranch."

"What about Mr. Jo..." Laura placed her fingers on his lips stopping the word.

"I think he'll still want to have you visit his shop. He wants to teach you to be a barber, after all."

"You think he will?" Hope sprang into the brown eyes so very much like hers.

"Yes, I think so." Laura smiled weakly. Hank was an honorable man. He wouldn't turn a boy who worshiped him away just because his mother was marrying someone else, would he?

~~~~~

Red was tying Ralph's reins to the hitching rail as Laura and her sons exited the house. She waved a bit and gave him a smile. Mark came running up and lifted his arms to be picked up.

"I want to say hi to Ralph." The horse was a White Paint with brown markings. Mark liked to talk with him whenever Red came to court.

"What about me? Don't I get a greeting?" Red lifted Mark into his arms.

"Sure, hi, Mr. Dickerson." Mark patted Ralph on the forehead.

Red looked at Laura. Had she told the boys they were getting married?

"I think under the circumstances," Laura said. "You can call Mr. Dickerson, Red. Is that all right with you?" She looked at him, her eyes pleading for confirmation.

"I think that's a mighty fine idea. What do you think, Eddie?" Red was under no illusion that Laura's older son was happy with the situation.

Eddie gave a wan smile. "Sure, Red. Mighty fine."

Mark hugged Red's neck. "Mighty fine indeed."

"Come along. We don't want to be late for service." Laura took hold of Eddie's hand, turning to follow the other ladies and children leaving the House and heading to church.

"Have you told your friends, yet?" Red figured she hadn't since no one came up to congratulate him.

"I thought we could do it at dinner. Is that all right with you?"

"Sure, it's fine." It bothered Red a bit that she hadn't shared the news but then, neither had he told anyone when he got back to the ranch.

They walked to the church and found a pew to sit on. Red made a point to sit next to Eddie. He needed to get to know the boy better. It was abundantly clear Eddie wasn't happy that his mother was marrying him.

~~~~

Red made sure he shared a hymnal with Eddie, allowing him to find the page even though they missed singing most of the first verse. He was rewarded with a quick smile. When they sat down again, Red laid his arm along the back of the pew behind the boy's head. When Eddie didn't react negatively, he took it as progress.

Pastor Preston came to the pulpit and said, "Today's Scripture is from the Psalms, chapter thirty-seven, verses three, four and five.

"*Trust in the LORD, and do good; so you will dwell in the land and enjoy security. Take delight in the LORD, and He will give you the desires of your heart. Commit your way to the LORD; trust in Him, and He will act.*

"So, do these verses mean that whatever you pray for, whatever you want, He will give to you? We all know that's not the case. We've all prayed, and the answer seems to be a resounding 'No.' We've lost loved ones we've prayed for. Had material losses. Disappointments. Relationships that are not what we hoped for.

"You've taken it to God and not found the answers you sought. Your faith wavers, doubt comes in. Then you think of the verses in James that say you do not receive because you doubt, and guilt sets in.

"But let us look more carefully at what the verses in Psalm thirty-seven say. '*Take delight in the LORD, Commit your way to the LORD, trust in Him.*' These are the key phrases, not the desires of your heart. God must always come first, be first in our lives.

"When we commit our way to the Lord, we are seeking His will and way for our lives. Our desires become what He wants, not what we want.

"Jesus spoke of this. We say it when we pray the Lord's Prayer. They aren't just words. They are powerful, life changing. '*Thy will be done.*' Not my will be done. Also, that we are to seek first the kingdom of God.

"So, what are our desires of our hearts? All through

Scripture, God says He doesn't want sacrifices. He tells Israel that their offerings are a stink in Heaven. He wants justice, mercy, kindness, humbleness. Above all, His will is that none should perish, that all come to the knowledge of the saving grace provided by Jesus and accept Him as Savior.

"I charge you to look at what you think are the desires of your heart. Are they in line with what God wants, or are they merely what you want?

"Trust in the LORD, and do good; so you will dwell in the land, and enjoy security. Take delight in the LORD, and He will give you the desires of your heart. Commit your way to the LORD; trust in Him, and He will act.

"Trust, delight, commit, seek His will, then He will act, and then your desires will align with His.

"Now, does this mean we aren't to pray for the things we want? Of course not. Verse four tells us He will give us the desires of our heart. We desire things that are both good and bad for us. We want security, love, the best for our children, prosperity, health, the health of our children.

"These are all in line with Scripture. But, it may be that we are to go through trials to learn what God wants us to learn so we can appreciate the blessings we have been or will be given. It may be that it's not the right time for our desire to be met. It may be God's mercy that makes it appear He's said no to our heart's desire.

"None of that changes the purpose of these verses. We are to examine our motives. Are our desires going to glorify God and His kingdom? Are they only for ourselves? Are they giving? Are they humble? Are they beneficial or selfish?

"Lamentations three, forty and forty-one: '*Let us test and examine our ways, and return to the Lord. Let us lift up our hearts as well as our hands to God in heaven.*' We need to test our ways, examine our hearts, and pray that our desires are pure. It's difficult, I know. That's another thing to pray for, eyes that see the truth of our motives."

Red thought about the words as they sang the closing hymn. Were his desires aligned with God's? He'd prayed to find a woman to marry, which he had. That her boys would accept him as a father. Well, that was a work in progress. That he'd earn and save enough to purchase his own spread someday. Were those wrong to pray for? Was he mostly to pray for justice, mercy, and that everyone be saved? He didn't think he was that selfless. He'd think on it a while, and maybe go ask Pastor Preston once he had the questions sorted out in his mind.

~~~~~

Laura couldn't get the sermon out of her mind as they walked back to the House. Had she prayed for the right things? For a successful business? A new husband? A father for her children? Was it wrong to pray for those? How could a sermon preached specifically on Scripture, with other verses to bear witness to the concept, leave her so confused?

Mark was pulling on her hand, begging to be allowed to run on ahead with John Basking. His mother was walking with him, so Laura released Mark to go to his friend. Eddie was walking beside Red, which made her glad. Maybe he was beginning to accept him as part of their family.

They hadn't talked about a date for the wedding yet. Laura didn't want it to be in the winter. She didn't know if Red would want to wait until spring. But then again, it was late January, and the cows were already beginning to drop their calves. Red had told her it was a busy time on the ranch. They rode out daily trying to find the newborns, making sure everything was well with them and their mothers. They needed to do the same with the mares. Any loss of life meant dollars worked for but not realized.

Eddie ran ahead when they reached the House yard. He, no doubt, wanted to get out of his Sunday clothes. The other children, especially the boys, were doing the same thing.

"Laura, how do you want to announce our betrothal?" Red's question sent thoughts of the sermon fleeing from her mind. He reached for her hand, holding it as they walked up the concrete sidewalk to the porch.

"I think over dessert. The ladies will be excited, and that will get the children worked up. We want them to eat a good meal."

"Sound plan. I'll leave it to you to decide the time."

By the time they got into the house, Eddie and Mark were thundering down the stairs.

"Did you put your good clothes away?" Laura asked. Both boys turned and started running back up. "That happens every week. You'd think they'd learn." She laughed, and Red laughed with her. *He really is a very fine man*, she thought. *I should be overjoyed that he wants to marry me. Please, Lord, change my attitude. Make him the desire of my heart.*

Those who had arrived before them were bustling around, setting the tables and beginning to bring the food in from the kitchen. Everything had been prepared and placed in the oven to bake while the service was in progress.

As soon as dessert was served, Laura tapped Red on the arm. They stood. All eyes focused on them.

Red cleared his throat. "Um, I'm not much for making announcements. Kinda scares me to death." Chuckles and giggles met his comment. "But this one I'm pleased to make. Mrs. Duffle has agreed to become my wife."

Libby and Gema clapped, jumping up and coming to give

Laura a hug. Ruth and Blanche followed a bit more slowly. Laura noted their smiles were more forced. She hoped Red didn't notice.

"When do you do the marriage?" Gema asked.

"We haven't set a date. Haven't even talked about it. He just asked me yesterday." Laura looked at Red. He winked at her. *Why, Lord, can't I want more to marry him?*

CHAPTER TWELVE

Hank came down the stairs from his apartment and noticed that the laundry room door was closed. Laura must be in there. When the barbershop was open, she closed the door to avoid the men who came to bathe. He wasn't open yet, so he wondered why the door wasn't open. The basket he placed dirty towels in was gone, so she was most likely washing them now. He ran his hand around the back of his neck. As much as he wanted to go in and chat with her, he moved on down the hall to the shop.

Noah's sermon had affected him in an odd way. He felt as if he had good motives for his prayers. He prayed for others more than himself and spent most of his prayer time praising and thanking God for his blessings and provisions. Was he not praying enough for himself? Noah had said it was all right to do so as long as you tried to place your motives within God's will.

Was he not praying for himself and his desires because he wanted God's will to be done in his life? Or was he afraid that his desires wouldn't come to fruition? The prayer of a righteous person avails much. But, what if God didn't answer the prayers for the desires of his heart? Or what if Hank never prayed for them? God, most likely, didn't just throw blessings at a person. Sure, he probably did sometimes, but we've been told to pray, asking God for what we want.

Hank stood in front of the mirror within the shelving above the counter, looking at himself. "Well, knucklehead, you missed your shot," Hank said to his reflection. "You had the chance at the desire of your heart, and you let her go to someone else. You can't even be mad or angry at the man. He's a good friend and an honorable man. Red will raise Eddie and Mark to be the same."

Hank brought his hands up and rubbed his face.

"Hank?" Laura's voice stilled his hands.

Pain gripped his chest. He knew what she was going to say. Words he didn't want to hear. He turned and leaned against the counter. "Morning."

"Good morning." Laura was at the doorway to the hall. She took a step further into the room. Her hands, clasped in front of her, were white knuckled.

Hank cleared his throat. There was a lump the size of a pumpkin in it. He tried to swallow it. "What can I do for you, Laura?"

"Um, I've got your towels all washed, and they are hanging now. They'll be ready in a few hours."

"That's fine. I have enough here." He lifted his hand indicating the stack of neatly folded white towels sitting on a shelf.

"Okay. Um." Now, Laura cleared her throat. He saw her swallow. "Red and I talked over the weekend. He asked me to marry him."

Hank was catawamptiously chawed up. He'd never felt so completely demolished, utterly defeated in his entire life. The lump in his throat split in two, and the biggest section landed in his stomach. "Best wishes on your marriage. Red's a good man. He'll make you a fine husband."

Hank saw Laura swallow again. Her eyes were dark and slightly sunken. They looked like two burnt holes in a blanket.

"Thank you." She shuffled her feet and twisted her fingers. "Well, I just wanted to tell you. I need to get back to my wash."

Hank nodded. He couldn't speak. The lump was blocking all his air. He watched her turn and head back down the hall.

Well, he'd best put Laura Duffle behind him. She was another man's now. He'd bungled the whole thing, and he had only himself to blame.

~~~~~

Laura closed the door behind her and leaned back against it. No, she wouldn't cry. Never once had Hank said anything that made her think he'd be interested in her. It didn't matter what her heart's desire was. The man did the courting. Women didn't make the first move or push themselves on a man. They were courted. They didn't do the courting themselves.

Red had come calling and asked her to marry him. Laura was fortunate to have such a good man want her and her boys. She'd do all she could to be a good wife for him.

Pushing off from the door, Laura took up the paddle and attacked the laundry in the tub with a vengeance.

Several hours later a knock sounded on the door. It opened, and Hank stuck his head in. "May I talk with you a mite?"

"Of course, come in." Laura set the flatiron on the stove.

"Laura, I've been considering. I'm thinking it might be best if you find a different place to run your business from. Red's my friend, and now that you're betrothed, well, it's a bit awkward for you and me to be here most of the day without anyone else around."

Laura's jaw dropped. It had never occurred to her that he

wouldn't want her around anymore. It felt like she'd been stabbed through the heart. "Of course." She turned around trying to think. It seemed her brain had just stopped. She picked up the iron and set it down again. What was she to do? "I'll be out by tomorrow, Wednesday at the latest."

"No hurry. Take the time you need."

"No, it's best if I get my things gathered and leave. Now, if you'll excuse me, I have to get this ironing done and begin to gather my things to remove them from your building. Thank you, Mr. Johnson, for allowing me to use your space for as long as you have."

Hank backed out and shut the door.

Laura placed her fist in her mouth and bit down on the keening cry that threatened to escape and fill the room with her sorrow.

~~~~~

Laura hadn't a clue what she was going to do. The weather was so cold there was no way she could work outdoors. She knew the ladies would allow her to use the washroom in the House, but that was something she didn't want to do. They had to be able to use the room for their own needs.

Daily, Chloe or Blanche washed and hung the towels they used at the café. Each of the ladies had a day they did their own laundry. Laura did laundry every day. There simply wasn't room or time for her to use the House washroom.

Hank had said there was no hurry, but she had no desire to be where she wasn't wanted. Maybe she could iron in one of the unused bedrooms upstairs. Each one had a small potbelly stove. Eddie could help her move her equipment.

Oh, Eddie was going to be devastated that he couldn't come to see Hank. Maybe she could talk him into still taking time with her son. At least until she married Red and they moved to the ranch.

Laura nearly ran from the room to ask him. Panic made her heart race. No, Hank hadn't said anything about Eddie not coming. He just didn't want her around anymore. She bit her lip. She wasn't going to cry.

She wasn't going to cry.

She wasn't going to cry.

If she wasn't going to cry, why were tears streaming down her face?

Well, if she was going to cry, she'd might as well do a bang-up job of it. Laura sat down on the floor, collapsed really since her legs had turned to mush. She reached into a basket of clean towels and pulled a handful out. Pressing them to her face she sobbed into them, muffling her cries in the towels.

When her tears were spent, she blew her nose, wiped her face, and threw the towels into the dirty basket. Hank would be short a few clean ones in the morning, but she didn't care. He'd be short for longer if she couldn't find a place to do his wash.

Standing, Laura shook out her skirts and pressed out the wrinkles in her apron with her hands, her shoulders stiff and her back ramrod straight. She had a successful business which could pay for room rental. The men would just have to wait for their clothes if she couldn't get them done on time. Most of them were cleaner than they had ever been before, so going a bit longer between washings wouldn't be a hardship. If it was and they didn't want her to do their laundry anymore, well, they could just find someone else.

Laura spent the time before lunch getting what laundry had been started done and hung up. Then, she emptied the tubs and began packing up her supplies in them. She would need help moving them as they were heavy. Well, Ozzie

Basking was thirteen. He should be able to carry them across the alley to the House.

Her shoulders slumped. Laura needed to tell the ladies that she had to find a new place to work. Two announcements in two days. She was looking forward to this one even less than she'd anticipated the last.

"Wrong attitude, Missy," Laura scolded herself. She placed the last bar of soap into the tub and dusted her hands. "Onward to your future." Taking her coat off the hook behind the door, she put it on, buttoning it against the frigid weather, and left the building.

~~~~~

"So that about sums it up." Laura and Ruth were in the kitchen doing the final preparations for the noon meal. The children would be home soon. They'd eat and then go back to school for the afternoon session.

"What are you going to do?" Ruth's eyes held concern.

"I'm going to find another place to do my work. There has to be someplace. I can afford to rent a spot. I really have too much business for me to handle." Laura thought for a moment. "Ruth, are you still looking for work?"

"Yes, I really don't like working for Mr. Bragg at the train station. The way he stares at me makes me very uncomfortable."

"How about you quit there and come work for me? We can work your hours around your other jobs. Maybe after school on the days you aren't cleaning. I've lost track. How many places are you doing now?"

"Well, I have Massot's shop and living quarters. I don't do much in the shop. He doesn't want me to touch anything. Mainly, I just sweep up the scraps and sawdust. His room upstairs is very spartan. It only takes me a couple of hours.

"Then I do the bank and the station. Mr. Ritter is very good to work for. He doesn't care if I'm there while the bank is open, but normally I'm not. That's when I'm watching John, Troy, Lil'Pen, and Abraham. Troy isn't all the time, or won't be once Leah comes back to the shop. Then, Myra will go back to part-time, I think. Next fall when school commences I'll only have Abraham. The three older ones will start school."

"It's hard to believe they are getting that old." Laura lifted the pot of ham and beans off the stove and placed it on a trivet on the table. Ruth got the pan of cornbread out of the oven. "What do you think of my idea of hiring you?"

"Can you really afford to pay me. I don't want to take money you need."

"You wouldn't be. You'd be helping me. You know how many hours I work. I even iron after supper some just to keep up. That's something you could do during the day. You do your own laundry while you watch the children, so why not be paid to do some more. We could set up some piece work prices. That way, whatever you had time to do you'd get paid for. If you didn't get it done during the day, it could wait until the next day, or we could iron after supper. It really would help me out." Laura grinned. "It would give me a reason to raise my prices too. That and having to pay to rent space."

"You didn't pay Hank?" Ruth asked as she filled the coffee pot with water from the reservoir.

"We did a barter. His barber and bathing towels washed for the room. Huh, he'll have to pay me now. Maybe I'll charge him extra."

"Laura, be nice."

CHAPTER THIRTEEN

Noah Preston looked up from his Bible as the door to his gun shop opened. He was surprised to see Mrs. Duffle standing there looking uncertain.

"Come in, Mrs. Duffle. What can I do for you?"

"Um, good afternoon, Pastor. Might I have a moment of your time?"

"Anytime, Mrs. Duffle. I'm always available. Please come in and close the door. We don't need to be trying to heat the outside." He placed a ribbon bookmark on the page and closed the book.

"Oh, of course, forgive me." Flustered, she stepped in and shut the door.

"So, are you wanting a firearm or is this a more pastoral visit?"

"Neither, Pastor. It's business."

Noah lifted an eyebrow. "Really? Do tell."

"You know Red Dickerson has been calling. Of course, you do, you're one of the men who have to approve the suitors. Well, he asked me to marry him. I said yes."

"Congratulations, Mrs. Duffle." Noah looked at her. She didn't look like a betrothed woman to him. There was little happiness in her countenance.

"Thank you. When I told Ha— Mr. Johnson, he decided that it might not be prudent for me to continue running my laundry service from his back room. It's too cold yet for me to work outdoors. I was wondering if, with your wife's approval of course, I could rent your backroom. It would only be until the weather warmed, and I can move back outside."

It seemed to Noah that Mrs. Duffle had shrunk just a bit. Or maybe it was her demeanor. Though she stood straight, almost as if she had a rod up her back and not simply a corset around her torso, there was an aura of tension laced with sadness surrounding her. What was going on with her? Noah hadn't a clue. He would have thought she would be happy with the news of her betrothal.

"I will consult with Vernie, but I'm sure she will not object. Would you like to see the room?"

"Yes, please."

Noah stood and lifted the hinged counter top to allow her through. He waved her to precede him and followed her down the hall.

Rather than having a center hallway with rooms on each side, his shop was only half as wide, so the rooms lined only one side. When they entered the last room, Laura made a slight gasp.

"It has two windows," she said with delight.

"Yes, a benefit of being on the end of the building." Noah surveyed the room. He'd seldom been in it. He only used the first two rooms. There was a stove that would work to heat the water. "What else would you need to be able to do your work here?"

He watched Mrs. Duffle look around. "I will ask Mr. Johnson if I can purchase the bench I've been using for my tubs. This room is smaller, and so I'll not be able to hang as much up. Lines will need to be strung."

"Come, let's look at this next room. I think it would suit your needs also. That room is about the same size. We could set this up as your drying room."

"I'm not sure I could afford to rent both rooms." Mrs. Duffle bit her lip.

"Don't worry about that. I'm sure we can come to an agreement. I'm not using the rooms, so you might as well."

They walked to the front of the gun shop, discussing the rental price.

"Thank you, Pastor. I appreciate your help."

"My pleasure, ma'am. I'll talk with Vernie tonight. Come tomorrow, and we'll settle up and discuss how I can help get those lines strung."

He watched as Mrs. Duffle's eyes filled. What was going on? She should be looking forward to a wedding and the move to Hawk's Wing Ranch. Instead, she was relocating her laundry business. There was nothing to stop Red and her from marry quickly. She could probably simply quit doing laundry for others. So, why wasn't she?

Mrs. Duffle was one of his flock. Having her working in the back rooms of his shop hopefully would allow him to gain insight into what was distressing her so. He'd be praying for her and for his ability to give her aid.

~~~~~

Laura picked up the twisted wet shirt, snapped it open and pinned it to the line. She reached into the basket and grabbed another garment, repeating the process. Over the past couple of weeks, she's settled into working in the back of the gun shop. Although the washroom was smaller, having the second room to hang laundry actually gave her more space.

There was one line in the washroom she hung small

clothes, handkerchiefs, and such on, but the rest went into the second room which was strictly for drying. She'd set her ironing board up in the washroom as well. Noah had hung several shelves to hold her supplies and flat irons. There wasn't the large reservoir for water she'd had at Hank's so she was hauling water more often. Pastor Preston hadn't thought of carrying water for her, and she'd never mentioned it. The rent he charged her was far too low for her to make such a request.

Snatching up a pair of trousers, Laura quickly pinned them. She placed her hands on her low back, stretching to release the muscles which were protesting that they needed a break. She needed a break from more than just laundry. Laura felt as if she needed a break from life.

Everyone at the House certainly needed a break from her. She was making everyone miserable. She seemed to constantly be in a bad mood. Small inconveniences and irritations didn't seem so. She was snapping at everyone, especially her sons. Just that morning she'd made Mark cry before he left for school. She couldn't even remember what caused her yell to at him. Whatever it was didn't warrant the scolding she'd given him.

The back door opened and the softly called, "Laura," made her reply that she was in the drying room. Ruth entered, carrying a basket of pressed and folded laundry. They'd worked out having Ruth do ironing with her being paid by the piece. It was something she could do while she watched the few children she took care of. Whatever she got done Ruth was paid for. It had allowed her to quit cleaning the train station for Ira Bragg. The young man made Ruth very nervous, with his buggy eyes watching her every movement.

"Here's Clem's things all finished. Do you want me to bag them up?" Each person who brought laundry to Laura had a large canvas bag with their name inked on it.

"Yes, please. It's in the other room." It was after the café closed, so Blanche would be home allowing Ruth to come help Laura.

Ruth left and returned shortly with another basket of clean wet garments. She moved to the next line and began pinning up the washed items. They worked in silence for a few minutes. The snap of shaking out each garment the only sound in the room.

"Laura," Ruth said finally. "Are you all right? I'm worried about you."

"I'm fine. Why do you ask?" Laura knew why and really didn't want to talk about it.

"You just seem out of sorts lately. That thing with Mark this morning. It's just not like you. It was just a bit of spilled milk. That would never have bothered you before. Why did it today?"

Laura finished pinning the union suit onto the line before she spoke. "I don't know. I just... I don't know, feel as if my insides are trembling all the time. Look." She held out her hand. "See, it's not shaking. Not at all, but my insides feel as though they are shaking like an aspen leaf in the wind."

"Oh, honey. Do you think you're getting ill?"

"No, it's not that kind of feeling. All I know is that little things bother me. They take on far too much importance. Like Mark spilling the milk." She gave a sad chuckle. "How often does he do that? At least three times a week? Maybe four? We wipe it up and go on. He's seven and a boy. He's going to spill some milk. He even gets a wet rag, wiping it up himself."

Ruth grinned at her. "Yes, he does. We've trained him well."

"He and all the others. 'Them what makes the mess cleans

it up,'" Laura quoted the phrase used at Sanctuary Place in Iowa and brought to Stones Creek.

"So, why such a fit this morning?"

Laura felt tears being to fill her throat. "I don't know. If I did, I'd know what to do to stop it."

"Is it Red? Does he make you nervous? Afraid?"

"No, Red's a gentleman. He's a good man. One any woman would be proud to marry. He'll be a good husband and father."

"But he's not the man you want?"

The tears slipped down Laura's face. "No."

~~~~~

Red walked into the gun shop. "Morning, Pastor."

"Morning, Red. What brings you to town today? As if I didn't know." Noah grinned at him.

"Well, I want to chat with Laura a bit and have some errands to run for Juanita. She's not satisfied with what's stocked in the way of airtights. Seems there ain't enough canned peaches, tomatoes, and grapes to suit her."

"How are the Valdez's? They settled in?"

"Seem to be doing well. Juanita's running the house well. Food's tasty too. Her tamales melt in your mouth until they light it on fire." The men chuckled. The Mexican couple had recently been hired by Hawk Connor as a housekeeper and stable master on Hawk's Wing Ranch. "I'm getting better at speaking Spanish. Alberto speaks English pretty well, but Juanita doesn't speak it very much. She understands mostly what you're saying but not always. Makes for some difficult times and funny happenings."

"I believe Laura's in the back. Thank you for giving me permission to call her by her first name. Seemed rather awkward to be calling her Mrs. Duffle all the time when she'll be Mrs. Dickerson soon. Have you set a date yet?"

"No, she wants it in the spring. That's fine with me. No hurry. Might even wait until school's out. Easier for the boys not to have to adjust to heading to town each day until school commences in the fall."

"Head on back. I appreciate you coming through the gun shop and letting me know you're here. We've got the men dropping off and picking up their laundry through here now too."

Red nodded and ducked under the counter rather than lifting it to pass into the back area and headed down the hall. "Laura," he said as he neared the rooms she used. He always did so now after he'd scared the living daylights out of Laura one time when he came into the room without alerting her.

"In here." The voice came from the far room where she did the washing and ironing. He went in. She was twisting some piece of clothing to get most of the water out before putting it through the wringer she'd recently purchased. Then he realized it was some man's union suit. That's what he'd come to talk with her about.

"I didn't expect to see you today. What brings you to town?"

"Pastor asked the same thing. Errands for Juanita, and do I need an excuse to see you?"

She smiled at him. "I don't suppose so, but you don't often come to town."

"I'm working, ma'am. Can't come and do that at the same time, mostly."

"That's why I was surprised to see you. You are hardworking." She twisted the unmentionables and placed them in a basket on the floor half-filled with other bundles. Reaching into the rinse water, she drew out another garment. This time a pair of denim pants.

"That's what I wanted to talk with you about. Your work, not mine."

"Oh?" Folding the pants over she held them over the rinse tub and began twisting the dripping mass as water poured out into the tub and down her forearms. Her sleeves were rolled up past her elbows, but he could see they were wet.

"I'm not sure I like you doing men's unmentionables. Doesn't seem real proper for a woman to be handling other men's…" he waved at the twisted red union suit.

"Comes with the territory, cowboy. Can't very well do a man's laundry without doing those." Laura ran the pants through the wringer.

"That's what I mean. I'd like you to stop doing laundry for other men."

"I can't very well make a living not doing men's laundry. I don't have women customers. They do their own laundry."

"I suppose you're right, but it just don't seem proper. At least you'll be quitting once we're married. Men won't come to the ranch to bring their washing to you."

"Maybe not, but there are the cowboys on the ranch. I can do theirs. I'll still like earning my own money. It'll contribute to our standard of living too."

"I make enough to support you and the boys, Laura." His voice had an edge to it. Didn't she think he could provide for her? The thought bruised something inside of him.

"It's not that. I know you wouldn't have come calling if you couldn't. Like I said, I like earning my own money. I can put some away for the future. If there's something I want, I won't have to use household funds to buy it. Won't have to ask for money to buy it. I had to with Alan."

"But…" he began.

"No, Red. You don't understand. There's no way you can. I

need to continue with my business, even on a more limited scale. When Alan died, I had nothing but what was in the wagon. I couldn't find work. I had about six dollars, not enough to keep me and two very small boys for very long. I nearly had to become a soiled dove because no one would hire me. If Nugget Nate Ryder hadn't had one of his Callings and come to the town I was in, I would have very likely resorted to that just to feed my children. I can't let that happen again."

Red watched as Laura became more and more agitated. She was pacing, wringing her hands, not looking at him. Then, she stopped in front of him.

"Can you guarantee you won't get killed in your work or by disease? Do you have enough money in the bank, so I won't have to worry about it if you do?"

"Well," he began.

"I didn't think so. You can take your improper for a woman to wash some man's unmentionables and throw it in a hog wallow!"

Laura brushed by him, going out of the room. He heard the back door open and close, leaving him standing, staring at the red lump of some man's underwear.

~~~~~

Laura flung herself across her bed and buried her head in her pillow. She hadn't thought of that time of grief and worry after Alan's death in a long time. Red's concern about her doing men's underwear in her washing had brought the fear rushing back. Until he'd told her to quit, Laura hadn't realized how important her continuing to take in laundry, even on a reduced scale, was to her.

She'd been very careful with what she earned. She knew, to the penny, how much she had in the bank. There was a ledger with each transaction recorded, all her income and expenses, both business and personal. Laura carefully budgeted for every purchase she made, and there was a tally listed as she saved for the rotary washing machine she hoped to purchase.

Always, she earmarked a percentage of her earnings that couldn't be touched as savings for the future. There would come a day when she couldn't work anymore. Laura planned to have enough saved to live on, and maybe to leave for her children when she passed. Never again would she be destitute if she could help it. Red not wanting her to wash men's clothing didn't hold a candle to her being self-supporting.

Also, having to ask for a bit of money for every purchase had always bothered her. Alan had held tight control of all their funds. He made the money, so he had the right to determine how it was spent. Laura wasn't a spendthrift, by any means, but purchasing the boys some penny candy or herself a new handkerchief, on occasion, shouldn't have to require permission from her husband. Having funds of her own would eliminate that.

The law gave everything she had to her husband once they married unless the man agreed to allow her to keep it. Laura hadn't thought about it before, but she was going to insist her bank account stayed in her name, even if it was a new name.

CHAPTER FOURTEEN

Hawk Connor, new owner of the large spread known as Hawk's Wing Ranch, rode along the fence line separating his place from the Tanner homestead. He'd met the man once. Silas was a sod buster, farming along the creek that gave the nearby town its name.

He looked over the landscape. Something wasn't right. He felt it in his bones. He didn't have Callings like his mentor Nugget Nate had, but he'd learned from the mountain man turned wealthy philanthropist not to ignore the feelings.

There. Smoke was rising just where the homestead was. That's what wasn't right. There was too much smoke. Sure, Silas could be burning a pile of trash, but Hawk was going to investigate anyway.

Locating a gate in the fence, he went through and galloped toward the smoke. When the homestead came into view, Hawk knew his instincts had been right. Something was very wrong here. Both the house and barn were on fire. A couple of cows were standing a ways off, looking at their former shelter.

When he arrived in the yard, Hawk yelled for Silas. Only the wind answered. The smell of burning wood assailed his nose. Coming from a campfire the aroma would be pleasant, familiar. This just had the smell of destruction.

Hawk dismounted, wrapping the reins around a post. The small cabin was less than a shell now. The barn still blazed some, but it wasn't threatening to spread. He looked at the trampled ground. Brown grass was trampled by a lot of hoof prints. A couple of pigs had been slaughtered and left where they fell. Chickens were scattered and clucking. A rooster stood on a post, crowing his displeasure.

Someone wanted this to look like Indians had attacked. The outlaws were a little light in the upper story. The hoof prints had shoes. Indians wouldn't waste food animals. If they killed, they took it with them. They'd have taken the chickens too.

Hawk figured it was the King gang, or whatever they were calling themselves now. They'd been setting upon farms and herds and towns since they'd arrived in the area last year. The leader, Buster King, and one other man had been captured in Stone's Creek in the fall.

A thirteen-year-old had held them at bay in the Creek Café after sending his five-year-old sister out the back door to get help. The men had been after their mother who was a partner in the café-bakery business. The King gang was known to kidnap women and use them in nefarious ways. Hawk wouldn't mind coming upon them and having them put up a fight. He wouldn't mind plugging them with a bit of lead.

There'd been a wife and a couple of babies when he'd visited before. She'd been a bit scared of him. His Indian heritage showing through. Hawk was only a quarter Hopi, but it showed in his swarthy complexion, black hair, and cognac colored eyes.

His grandfather, a French trapper, had lived with the tribe for a while in Arizona, marrying his grandmother and moving on to California long before gold was discovered. Their daughter had married his English-speaking father. Hawk was the only one of their children to live to adulthood. Growing up in the territory was difficult. Hawk had left home at sixteen thinking there was nothing for him there.

He'd traveled east, getting into fights and punching cows, until he met up with Nugget Nate Ryder. Nate had taken the angry young man under his wing, giving him a job and a chance to dig silver out of the mine that had made Nate a wealthy man. Nate let him keep what he dug. Between that and his wages as a US Marshal, Hawk had been able to purchase the ranch when he quit his work as a lawman.

Now, he was back doing a bit of that anyway. The US Marshal in the area had contacted him about keeping a lookout for the King gang and authorized him to use whatever force was necessary to bring them to justice. As he surveyed the destruction they'd left in their wake, he renewed his vow to do just that.

Hawk walked around to the back of the ruined cabin. He swore. There lay Silas Tanner, face down. They'd shot him in the back, the cowards. What had happened to his wife and children?

A sound brought Hawk's head up. That sounded like a crying child. Then a hush. He looked around. No, it was coming from beneath Silas.

The man lay sprawled near the corner of the cabin. Hawk strode up and turned the man over. A trap door had been hidden by the body. Blood covered it, but Hawk grabbed the ring handle anyway and pulled. Staring up at him from the hole in the ground was Silas' wife and two toddlers. She screamed, causing the little ones to cry.

"Ma'am, it's okay. I'm here. They're gone. Let me get you out of there." Hawk kept his tone calm. He held out his hand, after taking the bloody glove off and stuffing it in his back pocket. He waited, not wanting to scare her more than she already was.

"Mr. Connor?"

"Yes, Mrs. Tanner. It's Hawk Connor. Hand me one of the babes. I'll take you to Stones Creek. We'll find you a spot there. You can't stay here."

She took two steps up. "Here, take Arleta."

Hawk accepted the crying little girl and cuddled her against his chest. "Hush, little one. It'll be okay," he said in Spanish. The unfamiliar words caught Arleta's attention, and she quieted.

Mrs. Tanner climbed several more steps and Hawk held out his free hand to aid her out of the root cellar. He kept his body between her and her dead husband. He was glad to see they were all bundled against the cold. He wouldn't have had enough blankets to keep them warm. Fortunately, the day was mild for mid-February.

She stopped and looked around holding the back of her son's head against her shoulder. Then, she looked at Hawk. "He's dead, isn't he? Silas."

"Yes, ma'am, he is. You don't need to see. It's not pretty. Let's just head around to my horse. We don't need to stay. There's nothing here for you anymore."

She turned around, taking in what used to be her home and farmstead. "No, I suppose not."

As they headed to his horse, a whinny made Hawk turn, his hand ready to draw his gun if necessary. A saddled brown stock horse trotted across the lot to him.

"That's Pecos, Silas' horse. He smacked him on the rump when he saw the outlaws coming. He made me and the twins hide in the root cellar. I heard him telling them we'd gone to town and that he was alone on the farm. Then, I heard the shot and knew." She stopped talking and looked back at the burned shell of her home.

Hawk set Arleta down and took the boy from Mrs. Tanner, setting him next to the girl. "You two stay still. I'm going to get your ma on the horse first and then get you up there. Then, we'll go to town." Two very similar faces looked up at him. They were tear-streaked and dirty, but they obeyed.

Hawk lifted their mother onto Pecos. He picked up the boy, handing him to her. "You can ride, can't you? Or do you want me to lead him?"

Lifting a very shaky hand, she said, "I think you better lead him. I'm not sure I'd be able to control him very well."

"Okay. Hold this while I mount." Hawk handed her the reins, picked up Arleta, mounted, and took the reins back. He kicked the sides of his horse with his spurs and began the trek to town.

~~~~~

After tying up the horses, Hawk helped Mrs. Tanner dismount and picked up both of the twins. "Let's head into the café. I'm sure the children need to eat and so do you."

"I don't think I could eat."

"You will." Hawk knew his voice was stern, but she needed to eat to stay strong for her children. When she glanced up at him with a startled expression, he regretted his tone. "You need to keep up your strength. The days ahead are gonna be tough. Your young 'uns need you."

She nodded.

They went into the café, and he settled her at a table, placing each child on chairs pulled close beside her. Then, he went through the swinging doors into the kitchen.

"Excuse me. I need to talk with one of you ladies from

Sanctuary House."

Two heads turned to him. One was tall, thin, and had black hair. She lifted her left hand to her face, brushing a stray curl behind her ear. Her finger had a gold band on it. The other woman was more average in height. She had brown hair streaked with blonde. It was her eyes that arrested his intended words. They were large and green with depths like the bay of San Francisco. Hawk cleared his throat.

The green eyed woman spoke. Her voice was low and made something happen in the depths of his soul.

"What can I help you with?" She walked over to him, wiping her hands on a towel. "We normally come and wait on the tables."

"Yes, ma'am. I'm Hawk Connor, owner of Hawk's Wing Ranch. I'm needing to get some other kind of help too. I've got a woman and two young 'uns out there. The King gang just burned out their homestead and killed her mister. They've got nothing and nowheres to go. I was wondering if you'd take 'em in at Sanctuary House. I'm gonna be paying for their meal while I go and speak with the sheriff. I'd be pleased if I could tell him they've got a place to stay for a mite."

The women exchanged glances. "Of course, we can accommodate them for as long as they need. Let's go out and introduce ourselves, Chloe."

The dark haired one called Chloe was already moving to come into the dining room. Hawk stepped back, allowing both ladies to pass. He watched the sway of the hips of the shorter one.

She's not for the likes of you, Hawk, he thought, and went to introduce them. Or would have if he'd known their names and gotten there quickly enough.

"Hello, I'm Blanche Basking, and this is Chloe McIlroy.

We are so very sorry for your loss."

Mrs. Tanner looked at Hawk then back at Blanche. "I'm Lucy Tanner. I..." She stopped speaking.

"Don't you worry none. Mr. Connor explained what happened. We've come over to invite you and your little ones to stay at Sanctuary House for as long as you need. First, though, we need to get you all some food. We've got chicken and noodles, mashed potatoes, green beans, biscuits, and dried apple pie. How does that sound?"

Lucy just nodded.

Hawk knew she was in shock, but there was nothing else he could do for her. Blanche headed back to the kitchen. Hawk watched her go. He followed while Chloe McIlroy spoke softly to Lucy.

"Ma'am," he said over the swinging doors. "You keep a tally of what it costs to keep them. I'll pay what needs to be paid."

"No need, Mr. Connor."

Hawk interrupted. "Hawk, call me Hawk."

"All right, Mr. Hawk. There's no need. We'll make sure she and the children are taken care of. If there's anything we can't handle, we'll contact Nugget Nate Ryder. He'll be sure they can stay as long as they need."

"Right. I'd forgotten Nate sponsored this house like he does Sanctuary Place."

"You know Nate?" Blanche was dishing up one large plate and two bowls with mashed potatoes topped with creamy chicken and noodles.

"Yes, ma'am. Worked for him down New Mexico way. He got me out of a few scrapes."

"He does that for a lot of people." Blanche set the plate and bowls on a tray and picked it up.

"I'll be heading over to the jail now to talk with Sheriff Riverby. I thank y' for taking Mrs. Tanner and the little ones on."

"Not a problem, Mr. Hawk. We're pleased to be able to do so," she said as she passed by him.

~~~~~

Newt had just come back from having lunch with his wife, Myra and their son Troy. He was so glad he'd married her. She was a spitfire and flew off the handle a bit, generally punching or poking him in her ire, but he loved her. He'd heard back recently from the lawyer he'd contacted in Denver about adopting five-year-old Troy.

Newt had known Forsyth Franklin Fredrick Farnsworth the Fourth during the war. Everyone simply called him Four. He'd been the only man in his unit to survive the Second Battle of Manassas. He'd felt guilty for doing so, even though he was greatly wounded, losing a leg in the process.

Sitting down at the desk, Newt pulled out the letter he'd just picked up at the post office in Cutler's General Store. He was slitting it open when the door opened, and Hawk Connor came in.

"Hey, Hawk. Didn't expect to see you in town today," Newt said, laying his letter aside.

"Didn't expect to be coming. There was a problem out on the Tanner place. He's dead, the house and barn burned. I found the wife and young 'uns in the root cellar. Brought them into town. They're at the café. I'm buying them a meal. The House ladies are taking them in."

Newt swore. "We've got to catch these outlaws, Hawk. They're terrorizing the entire area. Wes found the remains of a steer they slaughtered. They took the best parts and left the rest to rot. Did the same on the Pactel place. Robbed a store in

Deer Trail. I can go on. Not to mention attempting to kidnap Chloe McIlroy last fall before she married McIlroy. We captured the leader and another man in that. Thought maybe they'd disband or leave these parts."

"Well, they didn't. I'll keep looking. If I find their hideout, I'll hightail it to town, and we'll get up a posse and smoke 'em out."

"Thanks for letting me know. I'll head out to the Tanner place with Dak, and we'll bring the body back for burial. Then I'll go to the House and talk with the missus. Let her get herself, and the children settled a bit first. Poor mites, no pa now."

Hawk nodded. There wasn't anything more to say.

~~~~~

Blanche walked with Lucy over to the House, each carrying one of the twins. She'd learned they were Arleta and Jack, fourteen months. Both were just on the verge of walking. Their pa would never get to see those first steps. Blanche nearly began crying at the thought.

"Let's find Ruth, and I think Gema might still be here. She works as a maid at the hotel. Ruth watches the children as their mothers work and helps Laura with her laundry business as well as cleaning a few places in town." Blanche knew she was chattering, but if she didn't, there would be silence as Lucy wasn't very responsive. "We'll get you settled in a room. There's a large one on the third floor across from mine. You'll be able to have the twins in there with you. It will fit your bed and two cribs."

They entered the back room with its dry sink and wash tubs. There were hooks low on the wall. A scarf hung on one, and a stray mitten lay on the floor. A few had coats and hats. These were the children's who were too young to go to school and who Ruth watched while their mothers worked. Blanche's son, John, was one. Chloe brought her daughter Lil'Pen when she came to work in the morning. Myra brought Troy on the days she worked at the dress shop.

They took off their coats and headed through the kitchen into the dining room. They found Ruth and the children there.

"Who have we here?" Ruth asked smiling.

"This is Lucy Tanner and her twins, Jack and Arleta. They'll be staying with us for a spell." Blanche looked pointedly at Ruth. She didn't want to explain the situation in front of Lucy. She was upset enough without having to hear it again.

Ruth gave a slight nod. "Welcome to Sanctuary House. How about we find you a room? These little ones look tired. I was just about to put these three down for a rest. Come along, now," Ruth turned her attention to her charges.

While Ruth settled Lil'Pen in her mother's old room, and John and Troy on Blanche's bed with the strict admonition to be quiet and rest, Blanche led Lucy into the largest room on the third floor. At the moment, sheets covered the bed, nightstand, and dresser.

"I'll go get a crib, and we can get them down for a nap. Oh, I'll get clean diapers first. We don't have any other babies at the moment, so they are put away. I'll be right back." She set Jack on his feet and quickly went to do her errand.

By the time she came back with diapering supplies, Ruth was there, taking the sheets off the furniture. Lucy stood where she'd been left.

"Here, dear," Blanche said. "You change Arleta, and I'll do Jack. We can change them on the bed since we'll put fresh sheets on anyway."

Lucy did as told, and soon the twins were clean and dry.

Lucy sat on the bed staring off into space, a toddler on each knee.

"Ruth, come help me bring a crib." Blanche waved a hand indicating she should accompany her. As they went to the store room, Blanche outlined what had brought Lucy and the twins to the House.

"Oh, my word. How horrible. Mr. Conner was right to bring them to you. Let's get this crib moved. I think there's another on the second floor. We need to change the sheets for Lucy. She needs to rest as much as the twins do. Do you have a night gown she can use or shall I get one of mine?"

"Mine's closer. I'll get it while you make up the bed as soon as we get the cribs set up."

Working as fast as they could, Blanche and Ruth soon had two cribs in the room with a sleeping child in each one. Ruth changed the sheets on the bed, and Blanche helped Lucy into the borrowed nightgown.

They tucked the new widow into bed, telling her she wasn't alone and that she needn't worry about anything at the moment. Just rest. Obediently, Lucy closed her eyes.

Blanche and Ruth stood side by side near the door and watched as tears slipped silently down Lucy's temples and into her hair.

CHAPTER FIFTEEN

The ladies of Sanctuary House, both single and married, rallied around Lucy and the twins. They gave or purchased clothing for all three. They held Lucy as she cried and comforted Arleta and Jack when they wanted their papa. Often, the lady involved cried with them. Each woman had known loss and tragedy in their own way.

A telegram was sent to Sanctuary Place telling of the addition. It also went to New Mexico where Nugget Nate would get the word. Letters giving more detail followed. A telegram was received back from their benefactor saying he'd wire funds to support Lucy until she was ready to get along with her life.

"I'm worried about Lucy," Blanche told Laura while they were doing dishes. "It's been almost two weeks, and she's still so docile. I had hoped the funeral would be a turning point, but she just moves through her day with no emotion. Not even the twins seem to make any connection with her."

"I know what you mean. She does whatever she's asked to do, but doesn't say hardly anything. Libby's taking care of the twins more and more. It seems to have helped Libby recover from her loss, but Lucy... I don't know. I think I'll ask Noah to come and speak with her." Laura handed the clean plate to

Blanche.

"That's a good idea. I know he talked with her before and after the funeral, but a visit now might be in order."

They worked silently beside each other for a while then Blanche said, "What about you, Laura? How are you doing?"

"Why do you ask?" Laura kept her tone impassive.

"You just don't seem very happy. You don't act like a bride normally acts. You don't seem eager to get married."

Laura wiped out the pan she was washing. "I don't know what I'm feeling. I'm just sort of numb. I thought accepting a proposal would bring peace and security to my life. Instead, I'm just anxious and nervous. The other day I didn't hear Red come down the hall. He always calls as he comes to alert me. When he came into the room, I nearly hit him with my wash paddle." She giggled. "You should have seen the look on his face. I apologized so much. I don't know why I'm so jumpy."

Blanche looked at her. "It's none of my business, but I have a question for you."

Laura paled. She didn't want to be asked if she really wanted to marry Red.

"Did you pray about Red's courting you and about whether you should accept his proposal?"

Laura's jaw dropped. It hadn't occurred to her, but she'd left God totally out of her decisions regarding the matter.

"Oh, Blanche, no, I didn't. How could I not have done so?"

"You want security and a husband. There's nothing wrong with that. Red's a believer, so thinking he was the right man or an acceptable man for you was understandable. God doesn't tell us who to marry, only that we are to marry a believer.

"But what if God has something better for you. Someone he chose for you and your boys? Remember when Pastor talked about the desires of our hearts. One thing stuck in my head. Maybe we have some learning to do so we can appreciate the desires of our hearts more. That maybe we need to wait on Him and His time to bless us.

"All I know is that you don't have peace, any kind of peace, let alone the peace that passes understanding. You may need to spend some time on your knees in order to get it."

~~~~~

Laura set the night candle on the dresser and opened the top drawer. Taking her Bible out, she gathered the candle and set it on the nightstand. She opened the Bible to Psalm thirty-seven. *Trust in the Lord, and do good;*
so you will live in the land, and enjoy security.
Take delight in the Lord,
and He will give you the desires of your heart.
Commit your way to the Lord;
trust in Him, and He will act.

Laura remembered the sermon Noah had preached on the passage. Trust in the Lord. Delight in the Lord. Commit to the Lord. The concept was to put God first. Want what He wants. Focus on Him. He has plans for you, plans for your good. That was a verse in Jeremiah. She'd have to find it.

She'd been so lonely and scared after Alan died. Nugget Nate and Sanctuary Place had given her a safe place to live for five years. Then the opportunity to come to Stones Creek and maybe find a new relationship arose, and with it the possibility for a new husband and the security that comes with it. Yes, Laura liked her independence, but the workload of the business and the boys and the House was a heavy burden. Even with the other ladies in the House, she was alone.

It is not good that man should be alone. That went for women too. Not only did she miss the security and companionship marriage provided, but she also missed the physical intimacy. Sometimes she ached with the lack. She'd hoped to develop a physical desire for Red, but it wasn't happening. Laura didn't think Red was burning with passionate desire either. At least his kisses didn't seem very hungry.

Setting the Bible on the nightstand, she stood and began to undress. She contemplated as she folded her garments away. Once she was in her nightgown, her hair braided and hanging down her back, she sank to her knees.

Tears streamed down her face as she poured out her sorrow at looking for security in someone besides her Savior. Warmth flooded her soul. Assurance of forgiveness filled her. She laid her torso across the bed and wept with thanksgiving. Peace began a gentle rain on her spirit.

When her tears ended, Laura humbly approached the throne, seeking confirmation that God's will for her was to marry Red Dickerson. Clarity is what she asked for. To know without a doubt. Either way, Laura was going to accept what God's plan for her was.

She thanked Him for the answer He was going to reveal to her and slowly got up. Drawing back the covers, Laura slipped into bed and snuggled into the warmth.

She slept more soundly than she had in weeks.

~~~~~

It was Saturday morning, and Laura was folding the last of Hank's towels. She was going to get ready for an outing with Red and the boys after dropping them off at the barbershop. He was coming to town to take them all out to the ranch.

Laura supposed it was about time, too. They hadn't been out there yet, nor had she met Hawk Connor, Red's boss.

No confirmation from the Lord had come yet either. Laura was trying to be patient and wait until He chose to let her know for sure whether she should continue with her betrothal or not. What she did know was that He would answer, in His time, and whatever it was would be the best thing for her.

She picked up the bag containing the towels and went through the gun shop, heading toward the boardwalk in front of the shops lining the block.

"Morning, Pastor." Laura set the bag on the counter, lifted the hinged section, went through, twirled around to close it again, and grabbed the bag.

"Morning, Laura. You seem chipper this morning." Noah was sorting small boxes of bullets in the corner.

"I am. It's a lovely day out."

"I'm glad to see you feeling happy. I was concerned about you there for a while."

Laura paused as she headed for the door. She turned and looked at Noah. "I was struggling there for a bit. I finally took my problem to the Lord and laid it at His feet. Now I'm just waiting for the answer so I can do what He wants me to do."

"Very good plan."

She exited the gun shop and went next door to the barbershop. She opened the door and heard arguing. In the hall leading to the bathing rooms, Hank and Red's voices were raised in anger.

"I thought you were my friend, but you're undermining my chances with Eddie."

"I am your friend, but I'm his too. He's not had a father for a long time."

"That's the role I'm supposed to be taking."

"I'm only mentoring the boy. He enjoys learning about barbering. I'm sure it will wain once he gets out on the ranch, and you get him a horse."

"That's just it. I went to talk with him this morning, hoping to spark his interest in our trip to the ranch today. You know what he said? Eddie told me he wasn't going to move to the ranch with us. He was going to stay in town and live with you. That you'd said he could."

"What? Well…"

"That's what he said. I'm telling you, Hank. I'll cut him off entirely from you if you don't back off. He's going to live with us, and I'll keep him from coming to town at all."

"What does Laura say about this?"

"I don't care what she has to say about it. I'm the man. What I say goes."

Laura couldn't believe what she was hearing. Red was taking over control of her sons? He didn't have the right, at least not yet. Even once they were married, she still had the final say in what happened with them. That Red thought he could make such decisions without even consulting her was appalling.

She flung the bag of towels onto the barber chair and stalked down the hallway, right up to Red, smacking him on the chest.

"Well, sir, you may not think I have any say in the matter, but let me tell you. I do! I'm still their mother, and I've been raising them alone for neigh on six years. I don't need you thinking you know what's best for my sons, especially without consulting me.

"Looks like I'm going to be continuing raising them alone, because any man who thinks I don't have any say in raising my sons doesn't deserve the right to do so. Mr. Dickerson, I hereby break our betrothal."

She wheeled around and stabbed Hank with her finger. "And you, telling Eddie he could come and live with you. How dare you say such a thing, or even imply it? He's a little boy.

He believes everything you say. You know he's been struggling with the move. You know. I trusted that you would support and help him adjust.

"I'd like to say Eddie can't come and see you anymore but that would be punishing him for your stupidity." Laura stepped back and looked at both of them. "Humph, now I have to go and tell both my sons that not only are we not going to the ranch today, but we won't be going at all. That you," she pointed at Red. "And I aren't getting married." Next, she pointed at Hank. "And you are otherwise engaged for the next week. In that time, you'd better come up with a good way of telling Eddie you were just plain stupid to tell him he could come and live with you.

"I'm ready to chuck you both in the washtub and scrub that foolishness right out."

Flipping her skirts behind her, Laura turned away from them, marched down the hall and out the back door, closing it with a resounding slam.

Hank and Red looked at each other.

"She's madder than an old wet hen," Red said.

"That she is. And she gave you the mitten," Hank replied.

"That she did. Think I have any chance of winning her back."

"Doubt it. That was a mite knuckle-headed thing to think, let alone say, even if you didn't know she was there."

"Yeah, I know. I got a mad on, and it fell out of my mouth without passing through my brain." Red ran his fingers through his hair. "You were fairly mush-headed, too. Telling the boy he could come live with you."

"It wasn't quite like that, but I can see how he might take it that way. I told him he could come and stay sometimes. I meant overnight, maybe on a Saturday. You'd be coming on

Sunday for service and could take him home after."

"He told me you wanted him to come and live with you."

"Guess I wasn't quite clear enough." Hank rubbed the back of his neck.

"Laura's pretty mad at both of us."

"Yeah, she is."

~~~~~

Once again, Laura gathered the boys on either side of her on the bed. This time wasn't any easier than the others. She wrapped an arm around each of their shoulders. She didn't know which bit of news to tell first. That she was no longer betrothed, or that Eddie wasn't going to see Hank for a week and that he wasn't going to go live with him.

"What's going on, Ma?" Eddie asked searching her face intently. "Mr. Red came today, and we talked about moving to the ranch. Then, he got mad and left real quick like."

"Did you tell him you were going to live with Mr. Hank?"

Eddie turned red and looked down. He picked at the quilt they were sitting on. "He told me I could. He told me I could come and stay whenever I wanted."

"And you thought that meant forever?"

"Well, maybe not forever, but lots."

"I see."

Laura was silent for a while. What she was going to say next would make one son happy and devastate the other. Mark truly liked Red and was excited at the prospect of moving to the ranch and having a horse. That wasn't going to happen now.

She tried to think of a way to salvage the situation, but there just didn't seem to be one. Lord, help her explain in a way that didn't reflect badly on Red. He wasn't a bad man, just chuckleheaded. When she thought about it, she knew he really didn't mean what he'd said. But that didn't mean she wanted him back.

"I've got some news that's basically sad. Mr. Red and I decided it was best if we don't get married."

"What?" Both boys said the word at the same time. One tone was stricken, the other delighted.

"We decided we simply didn't suit and that it was best to cancel the betrothal and go our separate ways."

"But why? Doesn't Mr. Red like me or want me?" Mark's small, sad questions broke Laura's heart.

"Mr. Red likes you real good. It's not you. It's between him and me. We just don't think we'll get along well enough to get married. I'm hoping we can still be friends."

Mark was silent. Laura leaned up a little so she could see his downturned face. Tears were streaming down his small cheeks. "I hope so too. Maybe then I could still go to the ranch and ride a horse."

"Maybe."

Laura looked at Eddie. There was a pensive look on his face. She patted his leg. "What are you thinking?"

"Is it 'cause I told him I was going to live with Mr. Hank?"

"You didn't cause this. What happened was God's way of saying He has something better planned for us. We just have to be faithful and believe that, and wait until He reveals it to us."

~~~~~

Red walked slowly up the walk to the porch of the House. He couldn't leave town without talking to Mark, especially, as well as Eddie and Laura. He had a lot of thinking to do. But he needed to clean up his mess first.

He knocked on the door. The young woman he'd seen crossing the street from the hotel answered. He'd been introduced to her the day he and Laura had announced their engagement. She was very pretty, young, with pale blonde hair and her blue eyes had an intriguing slant. He couldn't remember her name. Was it Jenny? Her last name was something he'd never be able to pronounce. Volko-something.

"Zdravstvujtye, greetings. You are here see Laura, yes?" She pulled the door wide to allow him entrance. "Come, in here." She pointed to the parlor.

Red went in and sat down while she went upstairs. The patter of youthful footsteps came running down the stairs. Mark flew around the corner and leaped into his lap. When he turned his face up, Red could see he'd been crying. His thoughtless comment had resulted in him hurting the boy.

"Ma said you and her aren't getting married."

Red could tell Mark was hoping he'd deny it. "That's right. We've decided it was best that we don't."

"That's what she said. Was it something I did?"

Red pulled Mark to him in a hug. "No, son. You did everything right. Sometimes adults think things are supposed to go one way when, really, God wants them to go another. That's what happened here."

"Can I still be your friend?"

"Of course, you're my partner, my buddy."

"But you won't teach me to ride or give me a horse." Disappointment about this was more evident than about the lack of the marriage. Red gave a half grin. "I can't give you a horse but, if your ma approves, I might be able to teach you to ride."

Mark pulled back and looked up into Red's face. "Really?"

"Really, but not for a while. I'm going to be heading into the hills on the back part of Hawk's Wing. I need to see if there are any cows that wandered that far in the winter."

"But it's still winter."

"Yeah, it is, but spring's coming real soon."

Eddie came into the room and stood next to the door.

"Mark, you go on now so I can talk with your brother a bit." Red set Mark on his feet and patted his back. "Go on." Mark ran off, and Red stood.

"Eddie, I'm hoping we can still be friends. Or maybe become friends." Red took a step but stopped when Eddie leaned back.

"Are you mad at me?" Eddie asked.

"Nothing to be mad at you for. Everything is between me and your ma. She's a mighty fine woman, and you need to listen to her and obey."

"I will."

"You take good care of her. Even though we aren't getting married, I think right highly of your mother. I'd hate to hear you were giving her heartache."

"I won't."

"Good. Um, is your mother going to come and talk with me or should I just go?" Red asked.

"She's coming. Wanted to freshen up some."

They both heard footsteps coming down the stairs.

"Go on now, Eddie. I want to talk with your ma in private."

Eddie nodded and headed out the door just as Laura entered.

She stood in the corner looking at him.

"Laura, I'm sorry. I didn't mean what I said. I was mad and jealous of Hank's relationship with Eddie. I should have been glad Eddie has a man who cares so much about him."

She nodded but didn't speak.

"I've done just a bit of thinking before I came over. Hank

let me sit in your old washroom. We're friends again, by the way. Shared moments of mutton-headedness does that between men. Puts us back on common ground."

Laura smiled a little.

"I'm not here to ask you to take me back. I realized it's most likely best we don't. I'm not saying you aren't a woman any man wouldn't be proud to have as a wife, but I... Well, this is for the best."

She nodded.

"I'm hoping we can be friends. I count you as one. And, I'd like to keep up with Mark. I'd like to teach him to ride. He really wants to. I could take him some on my days off."

"That's fine. You are an honorable man. One who will be a good example for Mark. I appreciate you wanting to stay in his life. He'll love learning to ride with you."

"Thanks. Laura, I only want the best for you. I realize that I'm not it."

"I'm not the best for you either, and I only want the best for you. I hope we can be friends."

"I don't see why not." Red walked to her and bent down to kiss her cheek. "I told Mark I'm heading up to the back part of the ranch to look for strays. It's true. I'm going to. I need time to think. Hawk will let me go for a while. It's something that needs to be done."

"Thank you for telling me. Now I won't worry when I don't see you at church."

Red put his hat on. "Goodbye, Laura."

"Goodbye, Red. God speed."

~~~~~

Hawk came out of the stable when Red rode into the lot. "Where's your lady and her boys? I thought you were bringing them out to see the place today."

"She gave me the mitten."

Hawk gave a low whistle. "Mind if I ask what happened?"

Red explained as he unsaddled and rubbed down Ralph. When he was done, he asked, "Is it all right with you if I head up to the line shack for a bit? I'll check the area for strays. I've got some thinking to do, and I'd just as soon do it alone. Alberto can handle anything here, and you can send someone for me if I'm needed."

"Sure, but I want you to do something while you're up there. I was going to head that way myself. With you going, I can do some other searching."

"Whatcha need me to do?"

Hawk explained about the King gang and his work with Sheriff Riverby and the US Marshals. Red was surprised that Hawk had been one himself. He'd never mentioned it before.

"I've kept it under my hat so as not to alert the outlaws there's an experienced Marshall in these parts. I'd appreciate you doing the same. If you catch wind of them, don't try to apprehend them yourself. You'll just end up dead. Hightail it back here, and we'll get up a posse to round 'em up."

"Will do. I'm gonna go and pack up my war bag and get Juanita to gather me some airtights, beans, and bacon. Once that's done, I'll take Milly as my pack mule and head out on Ralph."

Hawk laughed. "You really want to take that stubborn ole' donkey. She'll give you nothing but fits."

Red chuckled. "Might teach me a thing or two about women I need to learn."

"She just might at that."

CHAPTER SIXTEEN

Laura looked at Eddie and Mark. They hadn't eaten their supper well, which was highly unusual. They just sat there. Both boys were listless and slightly flushed. Reaching out, she laid a hand on Mark's cheek. It was warm.

"Honey, are you feeling okay?" Laura gathered him into her arms from his chair next to her.

"My head hurts." Mark coughed and looked up at her. His eyes were red and teary.

"How about we get you to bed? Hopefully, you'll feel better in the morning." She stood with Mark in her arms. "Eddie, you don't look like you feel good either."

Eddie sneezed. "I don't, Ma. I'm cold."

She placed her hand on his cheek too. It was hot. "Come on, let's get you tucked in, too."

Both boys were hot. She prayed it was just a cold coming on. This time of year always seemed to bring them. Living in the House, and previously the Place, diseases often spread quickly.

After settling the boys, Laura went back downstairs. "Both boys have a fever. Do any of your children seem ill?" she asked when she entered the kitchen. Blanche and Ruth were there, along with Libby.

"I didn't notice, and no one has complained," Blanche said. She had four children ranging in age from thirteen down to six.

Ruth's daughter, Kathryn, brought the last of the supper dishes into the room. "How do you feel, Kathryn?" she asked.

"Fine," the girl said. "Why?"

Laura told of her boys' fevers.

"Seth Cutler and Steven Hayes went home from school today, sick. Junior Brooks didn't look too good after school. He didn't stay around and pester anybody like he normally does."

The women all looked at one another. Each knew of someone who had lost children to epidemics. It was too early to tell if this was anything more than simple spring colds, but, with at least two children in the House and three others from school becoming ill on the same day, it just might be the portent of something serious. Laura knew she'd be spending some time praying this evening for health for all those of the House, Stones Creek, and the surrounding ranches.

She got up in the night and went into the bedroom Eddie and Mark shared. Eddie was coughing, and Mark was tossing, tangling his covers around him. Eddie wouldn't be going to school in the morning.

When she went back into the hall, Blanche was coming down the stairs, a night candle in her hand. "John's complaining that he doesn't feel well. His nose is running, and he's hot. I'm going to get some rags and a basin of water."

Laura wiped a hand down her face. "I don't think this is just a spring cold."

"Neither do I," Blanche said. Laura watched as she headed down to the first floor, the faint light from the candle fading as she went.

~~~~~

In the morning, both Eddie and Mark were feverish, coughing, had weepy red eyes, and just felt terrible. Laura ran over to the gun shop and told Noah she wouldn't be doing any laundry today or probably tomorrow. She hoped they only had bad colds, but Laura had a sinking feeling about whatever this illness was.

By the end of the following day, Blanche had called Doc Eli over. His diagnosis; Measles. Along with Laura's boys, Blanche's John and Nancy, and Gema were all sick with fevers, coughs, and sneezing. The red rash of measles began appearing. News came to the House that the epidemic was spreading through the children of Stones Creek and the adults who hadn't had the dreaded disease.

Laura didn't know if she'd had it since she couldn't remember. She tended Eddie and Mark as well as Blanche's two sick ones, Gema also.

The ladies labored bringing beds down to the second floor, and the children were all placed in one room. They were never left alone. If Laura wasn't there, Libby or Ruth were. Blanche helped when she could after she came home from the café.

Lucy and the twins were sequestered on the third floor in the hopes they wouldn't be exposed, though no one thought the twins would escape the infection. The ladies were concerned about Lucy, too. She'd not recovered from the shock of the attack on her homestead and death of her husband.

Laura, while not doing laundry for her customers, was kept busy doing it for those who were sick. Daily she did several loads of sheets, towels, rags and night clothes. Surfaces were wiped down with a mixture of vinegar and baking soda.

Five days in, Lucy came downstairs holding Arleta. The baby was listless, with a runny nose.

Ruth took the feverish child from her mother. "Lucy, I'll take care of her. You stay with Jack."

Lucy nodded and turned to head back up the stairs, took three steps, and collapsed in a heap.

"Libby, Laura," Ruth called. Libby came out of the sickroom and Laura's footsteps could be heard running up the stairs. "Lucy's sick. She didn't say anything. She just gave me the baby and turned back, then fell unconscious."

"I'll run up and get Jack," Libby said as she mounted the stairs to the third floor.

"We're going to need the cribs." Laura was nearly in tears. She was exhausted. All the ladies were who had the care of those who were sick. None of them were getting enough sleep. She was fortunate to be able to just say she wasn't taking laundry until the epidemic was over. Ruth was still cleaning the bank. Massot had told her she could skip his place until everyone was well. "I'm not sure I have the strength to bring them down. I'm simply too tired." Laura rubbed her eyes.

"I know," Ruth said, swaying back and forth as she held Arleta. "I'm not sure any of us could right now."

Laura knew it wasn't allowed, but said, "I'm going to get Hank. I know he's not supposed to be up here, but we need him to move the beds." Without waiting for a reply, she ran down the steps and out the back door.

~~~~~

Hank had kept an eye on the House ever since he'd heard about the epidemic. He'd made sure the wood box was always filled. He doubted the ladies even knew he was doing it. Not that he cared. He'd never tell them either. Don't brag about what you do for others, just do what's right because it's right. This was right.

He tossed and turned at night, praying for the little ones

who were sick. When he heard that the pretty Russian girl had fallen ill, Hank began praying for her, too. There was a light burning in the House all night. Someone was always awake tending those who were ill.

The back door to his building opened and slammed shut. Hank went to the doorway to the hall and saw Laura running toward him. He rushed to her and wrapped his arms around her, fear gripped him. Had one of her boys succumbed?

"Hank, we need help. We're so tired. Lucy and Arleta are both ill now. We need the cribs brought down from the third floor to the second. We just don't think we have the strength to do it. Will you help?"

Relief swept over him. As bad as more people coming down with measles was, she hadn't told him Eddie or Mark had died. "Of course. Let me get my coat. Laura, you should have put one on before you came over. It's raining." Hank took in her damp hair and clothing as he flipped the open sign to closed in the shop window. "It was foolish not to. You'll catch your death."

They'd gone to the end of the hall, and Hank turned to head up the steps to his apartment. "You stay here. I'll get my coat and something to cover you."

"But I need to get back," she protested.

"No, Laura, wait here. I'll just be a minute." Hank hated that his tone was so fierce, but she needed to obey. It was raining even harder now, the sound as it beat on the window told him ice was mixing in with the water droplets. She nodded, and Hank flew up the stairs two at a time.

Laura was leaning against the wall, her hands covering her face, when he jumped down the last four steps. He had his heavy coat on and carried a blanket and oilcloth.

"Here, let me wrap you in these." Hank pulled her to him

and wrapped the thick wool blanket around her shoulders and over her head, tucking the edges into her hands. "Hold this," he instructed, then he covered her with the oilcloth. "This will keep you dry."

Pulling her tight against his side, Hank held her close as he opened the back door. He wished they could wait until the storm eased, but knew she would never allow the delay. "Let's go. Keep hold of me. It might be slick. It's starting to ice."

They moved as quickly as they dared across the alley between the buildings. Ice was accumulating on every surface. Hank was careful not to let Laura slip and fall.

They shed their wraps in the washroom, leaving them on the floor as they entered the House. Hurrying through to the stairs and up to the second floor, they found Ruth and Libby trying to pick up Lucy who was still unconscious on the floor.

"Let me. You just tell me where to take her," Hank said as he bent to pick her up.

"In here," Laura said. "She can stay in my room. We don't have beds in the other rooms. Not ones that are ready, anyway."

"But, Laura," Ruth began.

"No, I'll manage. We can get some other bed ready before I sleep. Lucy needs to be close to the other sickrooms."

"Listen, it will be better if we have Lucy and Gema in the same room." Ruth took hold of Laura's shoulders and looked her in the eye. "I'll let Hank put Lucy in your room until we can get another bed into that room. It gives us time to get her changed into a nightgown, too. Then, he can carry her over. That way you'll have your room."

Hank saw Laura's shoulders slump. "You're right. I wasn't thinking. In here, Hank." She pointed to a doorway.

He carried Lucy in and laid her gently on the coverlet.

"Now, what do you need moved?"

Ruth and Libby closed the door behind Laura and Hank, saying they'd get Lucy changed. Soon, Hank was heading to the upper floor to bring two cribs down.

When he brought the first one into the large room they'd converted into a sick ward, Hank frowned. It was dim as the curtains were drawn tightly closed to keep the daylight from hurting the eyes of the sick.

The way the room was arranged wouldn't handle one more bed, let alone two cribs. He set the crib down in the hall. The two babies were on the floor. One lay curled on a blanket while the other sat sucking his thumb.

"I'm going to need to do some rearranging. There's no room."

Laura looked at him then at the beds. "You're right." She started to go in, but he stopped her.

"You get the babies out of here. I can't be tripping over them."

It wasn't long before Hank had rearranged the beds, end to end along the walls with the cribs in the middle. The space was crowded but would work. He'd placed a small table at the end of each crib allowing the ladies to have the supplies they needed nearby.

Hank stopped at each bedside after he was done and knelt, speaking to the occupant. That each child was quite ill was apparent. An angry red rash covered each face. Lips were cracked with fever. Sweat matted hair, and eyes were red.

Eddie and Mark's appearance clenched his heart. He knew them best, had come to love them. Losing either one didn't bear thinking about.

"Hey, buddy. You can't be shirking your duty. I've got combs to clean and floors to be swept. There's hair this deep."

Hank held his hand waist high.

Eddie gave a weak grin. "I'll get to it real soon."

"You do that." Hank touched Eddie's cheek with a gentle finger. "Rest and get better."

Moving to Mark's bed, Hank fought back tears. Mark's eyes were nearly swollen shut. He was coughing weakly. "Hey, cowboy." Hank caressed Mark's cheek. It was hot and rough from the rash. Heartened by the slight smile Mark gave him, Hank continued. "You get better real fast. I know when Red comes back, he's going to want to take you to the ranch and teach you to ride."

"You think so?" Mark asked.

"Yeah, I do. I've known Red a long time. He's a good cowboy. He'll keep his promise."

Mark nodded.

"Hank." Laura's voice had him rising to turn to her. "We need a bed moved so we can get Lucy settled."

"Right." He patted Mark on the shoulder and took one last survey of the occupants of the beds he'd moved before going to do as requested.

~~~~~

"You don't have to help with this," Laura protested as Hank hauled yet another bucket of water.

"Stop telling me what I don't have to do. I know that. I want to. Despite what I told Eddie about waist high hair clippings on my floor, business has been slow since the epidemic started. This is a way I can help."

Laura watched as he poured the water into the boiler. She had several loads of wash that needed to be done. It seemed that children's stomachs didn't handle fever and food all that well.

They now had six sick children, two of them one-year-olds

who needed constant attention, and two of the ladies. Libby had taken on the care of the twins, leaving the rest to Laura, Ruth, and Blanche, when she could get away from the café. Fortunately, Blanche, Almeda, and Chloe brought meals which removed the burden of cooking, but the dishes still needed to be washed.

They kept water going for tea all the time, trying to be careful not to let the pot run dry. Broth was warm in a kettle ready to pour into a cup to quench thirst and soothe throats.

Laura watched Hank head back out in the rain. It hadn't stopped in the hours since they ran across from the barbershop, though the ice had stopped and was melting. The alley and backyard were muddy messes.

Hank was doing so much to help her and the rest of the House occupants. He'd moved beds, carried Lucy, who was still unconscious, from one room to the other, gathered up laundry and brought it downstairs. Now, he was helping with the upkeep of the House.

The wood box was full. Laura was sure Hank had been keeping it so. She'd certainly never thought about it when she went to get wood for any of the stoves.

Tears flooded and threatened to overflow. Hank was so very good. He was so gentle as he'd moved the beds around. Sometimes he had to pick up the sick child and place them on another bed while he moved theirs. She could see his lips moving as he worked. He was praying, she just knew it. Praying for each child.

CHAPTER SEVENTEEN

"Lucy's awake. She's asking for you, Libby." Ruth touched Libby's shoulder, waking her as she sat in the sickroom.

"What time is it?" Libby rubbed the sleep from her eyes. The room was dark, lit only by the lantern set low.

"Just after three. Libby, she's worse. Worse than any of the others. Gema seems to be getting better. I know she came down with measles several days earlier, but she was never as sick as Lucy is."

Rising, Libby hugged Ruth. "Pray, that's all we can do. Will you stay here? They seem quiet, but you never know when the crisis will come."

"Of course." Ruth hugged Libby and released her to go to the other sickroom.

Gema was curled on her side, asleep, facing the other way. Lucy lay on her back, her eyes closed. Libby sat in the chair set close to the bed.

"Lucy, how are you, dear?"

"Libby, I need you to promise me something." Lucy's words were barely over a whisper. "I want you to take care of my Arleta and Jack. I need to know you'll love them like I do."

"Oh, Lucy."

"Please, I can't die without knowing they'll be loved like

Silas and I did."

"Don't say that. You'll recover. Fight. Please." Tears started to slip down Libby's face. "Don't give up."

"No, Libby. I'm not going to make it. I have no fight in me. I can't even fight for the twins." She paused, took a deep breath, and then coughed. "I'm giving them to you." Lucy raised a hand. Libby took hold of it. "I want you to adopt them. Make them yours." She stopped again turning her head to look at Libby in the dim light of a candle sitting on the nightstand. "I know you love them. I can tell." Another deep breath and cough. "Sell the homestead. All the property. Maybe there will be..." Lucy took another breath. "Maybe enough to live on. I don't know."

"Lucy..."

Lucy shook the hand she held that was lying on the bed. "Promise me. I can't die peacefully until I know the twins will be cared for and loved."

Libby laid her head on their clasped hands. "I promise, but, please, don't make me keep it. Please, Lucy, fight and live for your babes."

~~~~~

Laura looked exhausted. Hank studied her as she did yet another load of sheets and rags. There seemed to be a never ending pile of linens. She washed and hung all the rags they were using to wipe down backs and chests, trying to lower the fevers. Then she started on the sheets. Once those were done, she started all over on the soiled ones brought down from the second floor.

There weren't enough clotheslines in the washroom to hold all that was being washed. The weather wasn't cooperating to allow the outside lines to be used. Every day it rained off and on. Sometimes it was mixed with snow, sometimes ice. Never did the precipitation cease long enough to allow anything to dry.

Hank went to Cutler's store and bought hooks and line. He strung it across the end of the dining room after pushing the tables together, out of the way. No one was eating in there anyway.

He'd heard that several children had died, as had a cowboy from a ranch nearby. Noah and several other men were burying the dead. There would be a memorial service once the epidemic had run its course. School had been canceled until further notice.

Thankfully, the Cutler children weren't in danger though all three had contracted it. Noah's wife, Vernie, hadn't come out of their apartment since the illness had struck the town. Their daughter was only ten-months-old. Leah Steele hadn't either. Steven was only two months. Contracting measles that young was a death sentence. Eli was sleeping in his clinic rather than risk taking it home.

"Laura, you have to take a break. You're exhausted. Come, sit for a bit and rest. I'll get you tea and something to eat. Blanche brought baked eggs and sausages. Fresh bread, too." He placed a hand on her shoulder.

"These need to be done. I'll rest once I get them hung up."

"No, now, I insist. It won't hurt for them to sit a few minutes. It won't change their drying time that much." He took the rag from her hand and set it on the side of the washtub. "Come, sweetheart. For me."

Laura looked at him. Her eyes were bloodshot with dark rings beneath. Hank placed a hand on her cheek. It was hot, flushed. A fist clamped around his heart. She was sick. Burning up with fever.

"Laura, you're ill. I'm taking you upstairs and having Ruth put you to bed." Hank scooped her up into his arms and marched to the stairs. He hadn't been up on the second floor since he'd moved the beds around. She lay quiet, docile in his arms, her head falling to rest on his shoulder.

"I'm coming up," He yelled up the staircase. "Laura's ill." He could hear footsteps as he mounted.

Ruth appeared, concern written all over her face. "Oh no. Bring her in here. She'll have to stay in her own room. There isn't space in the others."

Hank followed Ruth and set Laura down on her bed. She was crying, and it made his heart hurt even more.

"I can't be sick. I have to keep up with the laundry."

Hank knelt beside the bed. "Laura, I know I can't do it as well as you, but I'm capable of washing sheets and rags. You need to stay in bed and get well."

"He's right, Laura. You just let us take care of everything. You get well. Don't worry about anything." Ruth stroked Laura's hair. She gave Hank a pointed look. "I need to get her into bed."

"Oh, right." He stood and looked at the very sick woman he now knew he loved. If she made it through this, there was nothing that was going to stop him from making her his. "I'll be downstairs if you need anything." Turning, he left the room, pulling the door shut as he went.

In the hall stood Eddie in his nightshirt and socks. Fear and despair warring on his face.

"Ma's sick."

Hank knelt and drew Eddie into his arms. He thanked God that both of Laura's boys were past the crisis. Their fevers had broken a couple of days ago. Though weak and still coughing, the rash was beginning to fade.

"Yes, Eddie, she is."

"Is she gonna die?"

A lump formed in his throat. Hank swallowed, trying to force it down. "She's a strong woman. A fighter. What we can do is pray that her measles are mild. Can you do that?" He wrapped his arms around Eddie and picked him up. "Let me get you settled back in bed."

"Will you stay with me? I'm scared for Ma," Eddie said as they entered the sickroom.

Libby was sitting in a rocking chair with one of the twins sleeping on her lap. She nodded at his inquiring look.

"Yeah, I'll stay for a while. Somebody has to do the washing though, and that task seems to have fallen to me. I won't leave the House though. I'll be near enough to hear you call if you need me."

Hank's heart nearly broke in two when Eddie started crying. When they sat on the bed, Mark came over and crawled up next to him. Hank wrapped an arm around him, too. What would he do if she died? He'd take these boys as his, that was one thing he was sure of.

~~~~~

Libby sat beside Lucy whenever she wasn't tending to the others sick in the House. Gema was recovering, though still weak. Laura was miserable with the fever and rash but trying very hard not to complain or be a burden.

Libby prayed and begged Lucy to fight, but neither God nor the young woman seemed to be listening. She also spent every moment that either of the twins were awake with them. She'd rock and sing to whichever she held. Sometimes she'd have both babies in her lap. And, though they filled at least part of the empty space in her heart, Libby wanted them to have their mother get well.

"Libby." Lucy's weak voice broke into her prayers.

"Yes, Sweetie?"

"Will you please get Pastor Preston for me? I want to talk with him a bit."

"Of course, I'll be right back. I'll send Hank to get him."

"Then bring Arleta and Jack in, will you?"

Libby nodded. She had an inkling what Lucy was preparing to do. She ran down the stairs and into the kitchen. Hank sat at the table there with a cup of coffee held between his hands.

"Hank." Libby's voice broke. She lifted a fisted hand to her mouth and bit on it to steady her emotions. "Lucy wants to talk with Pastor Preston. Will you, please, go get him?"

Hank slowly set the cup on the table. "She's given up, hasn't she?"

"Oh, Hank, she gave up days ago. I think she truly gave up the day of the attack. I've tried all I know to encourage her to fight, but..." Libby ran out of words.

"I'll be right back. Well, if he's at the gun shop. If not, I'll go and find him."

Libby watched Hank slip his arms into his coat, place his hat on his head and head out into the rain. She turned, went back upstairs and picked up Arleta, first, then Jack. Ruth watched as Libby carried the twins across the hall to visit with their mother.

~~~~~

Noah sat in the gun shop staring out the front window. This was one of those getting through times. He'd buried seven people, five of them children. He dearly hoped and prayed he wouldn't have to bury anymore.

Hank hurried passed the window and opened the door

entering the shop. "Pastor, you're needed at the House." The despondent expression didn't bode well for why he was being called for.

"Who?" was all Noah said. He understood what he was going to find when he arrived. Someone was either dead or dying.

"Lucy Tanner. She's been real sick, sicker than any of the others. The ladies say she won't fight. That she's given up."

Noah had already put on his coat. "Come on, let's go out the back. Less time spent in the rain."

It wasn't long before Noah was following Hank up the stairs, though his feet felt as if they were made of lead. Several of the children were gathered in the doorway to one of the rooms. Ruth stood next to Gema who was pale with the remnants of rash on her face. The young immigrant was in a dressing gown, her hands gripping the lapels closed.

Hank stopped at the door on the other side of the hall. "Libby, Pastor's here."

Noah moved into the room. Libby stood from the chair she'd been sitting in. The curtains were drawn, and a lantern burned low on a side table. Lucy lay on the bed. She was nearly as pale as the white coverlet spread over her. The twins mirrored each other, snuggling close next to their mother's sides.

A heaviness settled on Noah's shoulders. "Mrs. Tanner, Lucy, I've come as you asked. What can I do for you?"

"Thank you. Once I finish my business, I'd like you to pray with me and read the twenty-third Psalm. First, though, I want you as a witness." Lucy paused. She seemed to be struggling to breathe.

Noah waited. She would continue when she was ready.

"Libby, will you get Ruth, please."

Libby nodded and left, returning momentarily with Ruth.

"I've always been told that the words of Scripture are for us to use as our own." Lucy stroked the backs of each of her children. "Pastor, Ruth, I ask you to be witnesses. If there's any time in the future you need to lend Libby support, you can testify my wishes and intent."

Libby started crying, pressing her hand to her mouth to stifle the sob. She moved near the head of the bed and laid her hand on Lucy's shoulder.

"Bend close," Lucy instructed Libby. When Libby was kneeling, Lucy said, "Give me your hands." When she had them, Lucy lay one on Arleta and one on Jack. "Children, behold your mother. Libby, behold your children."

Libby broke down crying and laid her head on the bed. "No, Lucy. Please get well."

"I'm not going to, Libby. I need to know you'll take my babies." Lucy stopped. Noah didn't know whether she was struggling for breath or to contain her emotions. "You told me the other day you'd take care of my babies."

Libby nodded, sliding her head on the blanket. "I know. I will; you know I will. But…"

"Shhh. It's all right. I'm going to be with my Jesus and my Silas. You're going to be such a good mother to my babes." Lucy took a shuddery breath. She turned her focus to Noah and Ruth. "You heard my wishes. I don't have a will, but I want the homestead to be sold. Anything over the mortgage is to go to Libby to help keep my babies."

"Of course," Noah and Ruth said at the same time.

"We'll stand as witness to your wishes. Rest easy, Lucy," Noah said.

She gave a weak smile. "Thank you. God's given me peace." She lifted a hand and stroked Libby's hair. "I haven't known you very long, but you're like a sister to me. I love you dearly."

Noah took his Bible from his coat pocket and opened it to the Psalm Lucy had requested. He didn't need the book. He knew it by heart. In a calm, clear voice he recited the familiar words.

~~~~~

In the early hours of morning, with her children nestled against her sides and Libby dozing in the chair close by, Lucy slipped into the waiting arms of her Savior.

CHAPTER EIGHTEEN

Lucy's death cast a pall over the occupants of the House. Even the rest of the children and Gema on the rebound couldn't totally dispel the sadness.

Hank had gone to Massot and told him another casket needed to be made. The man had gone white and asked for whom. The color had come back into Massot's face when he heard it was Lucy Tanner, making Hank wonder who the taciturn carpenter might be interested in.

It better not be Laura. Hank had plans once she was fully over the measles. No longer was he going to be unsure or undecided about what, or rather who he wanted.

Three days after Lucy's death, Hank accompanied Noah to the cemetery. Chloe McIlroy, Blanche Basking, Myra Riverby, and Libby Trembly were all there. They stood silently as their friend was laid to rest. The others stayed with the recovering measles sufferers. Letters were sent to both Sanctuary Place and Nugget Nate's ranch, delivering the sad news.

Hank kept up his support of the House. He made sure the wood box was full. Gema was well enough to take over the laundry needs. They were lessening as more of the children improved.

School wouldn't start for another week to make sure

everyone was well and strong enough to return. Hank had Eddie and Mark come over to the barbershop for an hour or two every day to keep them from being underfoot, now that they had their energy back.

Eddie told him that his ma was not being a good patient. Ruth had to keep telling her to go back to bed. Mark added that she looked "really ugly" with the red rash all over her face. She had a "really big, ugly spot above her lip that looked like it just might explode like dynamite." Hank bit his lip to keep from laughing.

~~~~~

Laura was tired of being in bed. Her fever had finally broken, and the rash was beginning to fade. She'd taken a look at her face in the mirror once and quickly looked away. No need to see that again.

She was nearly afraid to get out of bed and venture out into the hall. It seemed that any time she did, either Ruth or Libby was scolding her, taking her arm, and escorting her back to her room. No wonder everyone was so weak when the illness retreated, they'd been doing nothing for over a week and lost all their strength lying around in bed.

Each day, Mark and Eddie would come running up the stairs, sounding like a herd of stampeding cattle, and swing through the doorway to jump onto her bed. They'd spent most of the afternoon with Hank and always had things they wanted to tell her.

Eddie was back to his old self, enjoying being with the barber and learning about the trade. Mark was becoming interested, not in the barbering, but in other things appealing to a young boy.

Hope began creeping ever so slowly into Laura's heart.

Maybe Hank would want a more permanent relationship with the boys. Even though he didn't seem attracted to her, two impressionable young boys wanting his attention might give him pause to think favorably about a bond with her.

Could she live with unrequited love? The question startled her when it parked itself in her mind. Love? Hank? Laura flopped back against the pillows. She was doomed. She was in love with Hank, but he didn't return her feelings.

Throughout the epidemic, Hank had been a bulwark; solid and stable supporting her as well as the others. He'd spent nearly every daylight hour at the House, normally by her side whenever she was downstairs. He'd carried water and wood, made coffee and tea. He went to the café and picked up the food the ladies there had prepared for those in the House.

When Laura fell ill, Hank had taken over washing the laundry. At least the sheets, towels, and rags. He'd drawn the line at the unmentionables and diapers. Ruth said he didn't prefer to do the nightgowns and nightshirts.

Throughout the entire epidemic, Hank had endeared himself even more to Laura. His willingness to help with little or no thought of thanks showed character traits she wanted to develop in Eddie and Mark.

Yes, she was doomed. Here was the man who sparked her heart with desire and love, yet he'd never once given any indication he felt anything more than friendship.

~~~~~

Hank stood looking out his barbershop window. The weather had finally straightened up. They'd had three full days without rain so the street was dry enough mud didn't cake on a man's boots when he walked across.

He'd heard that Laura was recovering. She wasn't

planning on taking in laundry until next Monday, but she was gaining strength every day. Hank had gone to the café for lunch and inquired. Now, he had to decide how he was going to proceed.

The way courting a Sanctuary House lady was supposed to commence, the suitor had to get approval from the men Nate had charged with the task. Hank could do that, he supposed, but he wanted to do something a bit more unique. Something that would tell Laura he was declaring himself not as just a suitor but as someone who had fallen in love with her.

Hank knew there wouldn't be any trouble with approval from Pastor Preston and the other men. A while back, Ben Cutler had asked him why he hadn't begun courting any of the ladies. Seems Hank was already approved, so now he needed to find a way to make Laura feel as special as he thought she was.

Hank slipped into his coat and, taking the broom, went outside to sweep the boardwalk. Sheriff Newt Riverby was making his afternoon walk around town. He climbed the steps to the walk by the café, came near to where Hank was sweeping, and leaned against the building.

"Afternoon, Hank. Weather seems to have sweetened a bit."

"Yep. Good to be able to walk out without getting drenched or your boots stuck in the mud."

Newt laughed. Then, he eyed Hank appraisingly. "How's come you've never courted one of the ladies, Hank? You've got to know you'd be welcome to."

"Well, Sheriff, I was just thinking that myself. Would you be so kind as to arrange for you and the rest of the committee to come and meet with me here at the shop tomorrow morning, say at seven-thirty? That's before we open our businesses and

Doc the clinic. We'd be able to have a bit of a jaw about that there topic."

"You supply coffee and some of Almeda's doughnuts, and I'm pretty sure I can arrange that," Newt said.

Hank laughed. "Can do, Sheriff. Can do."

Sheriff Riverby proceeded on his rounds, and Hank swept the entire length of the boardwalk, stopping in the café-bakery and ordering two dozen doughnuts for the next morning.

~~~~~

The sun was shining, promising another lovely spring day. Hank had a large pot of coffee brewing on the stove with five mugs on the counter. He'd picked up the doughnuts. When Hank had slipped up and mentioned he was meeting with Pastor Preston, Sheriff Riverby, Doc Eli, and Ben Cutler, Almeda had broken into a huge grin and added another six doughnuts to the box.

"That way you'll each be havin' six doughnuts apiece." As she handed him the box, Chloe McIlroy and Blanche Basking, who partnered with Almeda in the business, came through the arched doorway between the bakery and café.

"Morning, Hank," they said.

Hank touched a couple of fingers to his hat. "Morning, ladies."

"Hank, here, he's havin' a meetin' with the committeemen about courtin'."

"I never said that." Hank shot a glance at Almeda, who just grinned.

"Didn't have to. Havin' them men gettin' together only means one thing."

Chloe laughed. "That's right, Hank."

Blanche looked him up and down. "I've only got one thing to say to you, Hank. It's about time."

With three ladies laughing, Hank hustled out of the bakery and back to the safe haven of his men's barbershop.

Not long after, the four men arrived. Hank poured coffee, and each man grabbed a doughnut before settling in the chairs lining the walls of the shop. They sipped the hot, fragrant brew and each ate several doughnuts, chatting amiably.

"As nice as it is to begin the day with some man talk and doughnuts," Ben Cutler began, "I've got a store to open. So hows about you give us a clue as to why we've been called here."

Hank felt his face heat. He'd thought over what he was going to say, but, now that the time had come to actually let the words flow, he was nervous and embarrassed.

He cleared his throat, lifted a silent prayer to Heaven, and opened his mouth. "I'm, um, I'm fixing to ask Laura Duffle to marry me, and I'm wanting your consent to my doing so." Relief that he'd gotten the words out poured over him.

"Hank," Noah said. "That's not how this is supposed to go. Nugget Nate has us approve the men to begin courting. You can't just ask to marry the lady."

Hank's previous elation plummeted at Pastor Preston's comment.

~~~~~

Laura opened the front door to Sanctuary House, answering the knock. Hank stood there with his Stetson in his hands. He was circling it, rubbing the brim between his fingers.

"Afternoon, Hank. Why'd you come to the front? You usually come in the back door." She stood back to allow him to enter.

"Well, ma'am, Laura. I've come to ask…" Hank's voice broke over the next word. He cleared his throat and started again. "I've come to ask if you'd come and help me over at the general store? I've got something I need a woman's help in choosing."

"Of course, I'll help you. Let me get my cloak." Laura went up to her room, wondering what Hank could possibly need her help in picking out. He wasn't an inexperienced youth away from his mother for the first time.

She looked in the mirror on her wall as she pinned on her hat and studied her face for a moment. She'd lost some weight, which wasn't a bad thing, but she still looked rather pale. Oh well, nothing could be done about that. Laura thought about applying some rose water but didn't reach for the bottle. A little fragrance wasn't going to attract Hank after all these months.

When Laura returned, Hank came from the parlor he'd wandered into while she was upstairs. "Ready?" he asked.

"Yes." Laura led the way outside and was surprised when Hank laid a hand on her lower back and took her elbow as they descended the steps. "So, what is it you need my help with?"

"I'll show you when we get there. I want to know how you are feeling? Are you all recovered from the measles?"

Laura glanced up at him, noticing his intense gaze as he studied her face. "Yes, I'm well. I plan to start back working next week. I'm sure the cowboys will be glad to get their clean laundry back. It's been three weeks. I won't charge them extra for the next batch being far too dirty."

"They'll appreciate that. Though I must say, they were all very understanding and told me to give their regards when I saw you next. They were all worried about you."

"That's sweet. Though it may be that they don't want to have to do their own laundry again."

Hank chuckled. "Maybe."

He held open the door to Cutler's General Store and allowed her to enter before him. "Let's head over here."

Again, Hank surprised Laura as he took her hand and held it as they wove their way between the shelves. He led her to the locked display of jewelry. Then he turned to face her.

"Laura, you've come to mean a great deal to me. Will you marry me?"

For the third time in less than an hour, Hank surprised her. No, this time it was shock. "But, but, but," she stammered. "You haven't courted me?"

Hank gently took her by the elbows. "Laura, honey, what is courting? It's getting to know one another. It's seeing if we'd suit. It's spending time learning who the other person is and liking, no loving, what they see. We've been doing that since you first came stammering up to me, asking for my help in starting your business.

"I know. I was pretty slow on the uptake. I let fear of change, of taking on the responsibility of you and the boys, hold me back from declaring myself months ago. Then I nearly lost my chance, not once but twice.

"First, Red asked to court you and then you planned to marry him. After you gave him the mitten, you were so mad at me I thought I'd lost you for good.

"Then came the epidemic. You came to me for help. You could have gone to any of the other men in town to move those cribs, and they would have gladly helped. But you came to me. I knew then God was giving me one last chance to endear myself to you.

"Don't get me wrong. I would have helped out like I did even if I couldn't stand the sight of you."

Laura giggled as Hank moved his hands down her arms to

embrace her hands.

"During those stressful days, we worked together and, in my view, moved passed attraction and desire to love and commitment."

Tears gathered in Laura's eyes. She'd had no clue, or maybe she had just guarded her heart from seeing so she wouldn't be disappointed when they went back to simply being friends.

"Oh, Hank. I've wanted you for so long. Even when I said yes to Red, I really wanted you."

"Laura, I love you. Will you marry me? You can pick out your ring as soon as you say yes."

Throwing her arms around his neck, Laura said, "I love you, too. Yes, I'll marry you."

Hank melded his lips to Laura's, and she thought she'd never tasted anything so good. It took them both a moment to realize applause was sounding behind them. They turned their heads in that direction. Ben Cutler, his wife, Sara, Noah and Vernie Preston, Doc Eli and Leah Steele, Newt and Myra Riverby and Blanche Basking were standing there with grins on their faces, clapping.

Abbie, the Cutler's eight-year-old daughter, squeezed between the adult's legs to the front of the group. She looked up and studied Hank and Laura for a moment. "My papa said it was about time you two quit just making eyes at each other and tied the knot. You were kissing, so you'll have to get married now."

Everyone burst out laughing and came forward to congratulate the newly betrothed couple.

The laundry lady had found her love in the town barber, even if she'd had to climb a mountain of dirty clothes to reach him. All thanks to God, and with a little help from a crotchety old mountain man named Nugget Nate.

EPIDEMICS IN THE PAST

In our time, we don't understand the impact an epidemic had on a family or community. Measles, Mumps, Whooping Cough, Smallpox, Scarlet Fever, Influenza, Diphtheria, Typhoid, and more were all feared because of the death that came in their wake.

It wasn't that long ago that quarantine was used to help combat the spread of epidemics. When I was a child, my sister and I both had the measles at the same time. I can remember the red 'This House is Under Quarantine' sign in our window. That was in the 1960's. Vaccines have done much to eliminate these dreaded diseases.

The ladies' fear for their children and other adults was real. Any or most of the children of the House could have died. I probably defied actual occurrence by not having any of them do so.

A NOTE FROM SOPHIE

I hope you enjoyed **Laundry Lady's Love**. Please take a moment to leave a review on Amazon. For independently publishing authors like myself, the reviews are extremely valuable in getting our work noticed. If you take just a few minutes, you could help someone else find their next favorite book.
You can post a review right from your Kindle or Kindle app. Just scroll past the end of the book. The form will pop up. Although Amazon says they require 20 words they will post it with less. You can pad your review with the title of the book and author name.
Thank you.
Sophie
Continue on for the first chapter of **Music for Her Heart** the second book in the **Stones Creek - Ladies of Sanctuary House Series**.

Books by Sophie Dawson
Cottonwood Series
Healing Love
Lord's Love
Giving Love
Redeeming Love (With George McVey)

Stones Creek Series
Leah's Peace
Chasing Norie
Chloe's Choice (Short Story)
Chloe's Sanctuary
Love's Infestation
Mold and Marriage
Spots Before Marriage
Mice and Marriage
Java Cupid Multi-Author series
Java Priority #4
Single Books
Seeing The Life
Rescued By Love

If you enjoyed this book and would like to find other great Christian Indie Authors reads, follow the link below. Christian Books in Multiple Genres, Join Christian Indie Author ~ Readers Group on Facebook. Opportunities for free books and giveaways.

MUSIC OF HER HEART

CHAPTER 1

All she could hear was the blood pounding in her ears and the ragged intake and exhale of air as she ran. Gema Volkovichna didn't look back. She just ran. She had to get away. That woman, Flora, had sacrificed herself for her. Gema wasn't going to allow that to be wasted.

She hadn't a clue where she was going, just away. Away from the small cave, the group of outlaws was using as their hideout. Away from certain rape and abuse.

Terror drove Gema on. She tripped, nearly falling. She wished the clouds would break so she could see the sun. She had no idea what direction she was running. Was she heading toward Stones Creek or away? Were the trees thinning? If she left, the cover of the forest would they find her? Stones Creek was near where the land sloped up from plains to forested hills. Just past the edge of town the woods began.

If only she could get back to Stones Creek. Then she'd be safe. Or would she? She'd been kidnapped right from the street in the middle of the day. Or rather the alley behind the hotel where she worked as a maid.

Gema had left the hotel by the back door to go have her

midday meal at Sanctuary House where she lived. She hadn't been in the Colorado town long. Only since January. It was now late-March.

As she walked behind the hotel, Gema was grabbed from behind and flung over the back of a horse. Whoever was holding her across the saddle kicked the horse into a gallop before she could even try to scream. The saddle horn dug into her hip. It wasn't long before her hat lost its hold and fell to the ground. Gema hadn't a clue how far they traveled. She might have even fainted for a while.

When the horse was brought to a halt, Gema was dumped to the ground. Her blonde hair was streaming around her face and shoulders, the pins having long past lost their grip on the blonde strands. She looked up from her crouch on the ground and saw four men leering down at her. Grins that spoke of their intent stole her breath.

"Please, let me go." Gema knew they wouldn't understand her words. She'd spoken in her native Russian. Her fear made the use of English impossible.

"Well, girly, I ain't got no clue abouts what you're sayin' an' I don't rightly care. You're a fine lookin' piece, I must say. Nice 'n trim. You'll do us mighty fine." The man was dirty and missing several teeth. His beat up cap sat low over his forehead. Another man stood next to him. Licking his lips. Two more were securing the horses to a brush nearby.

Gema looked around, frantically searching for a place to run. She backed up. A rock cliff rose behind, stopping her retreat. What was she going to do? *Lord, help me. Please don't let them...* She couldn't even think the words.

"What have you done now?" Gema turned toward the sound of a woman's voice. A large boned woman in ratty clothing stood with her hands on her hips in the opening to a dark cave.

"We done brought us another woman. She'll take up what Prue used to do. Maybe some of Roda's tasks too, now that they's both dead." The man said.

Another woman came to stand behind the first. "No, Ornan. You have to take her back. They'll come after us for sure. What are we gonna do iffen we have to hightail it outta here? We've still got sick younguns."

More faces began appearing behind the women. Several children and young teens. All were thin, dressed in ragged garments and several had faces covered in a red rash. Gema knew what that was. She'd been ill for nearly three weeks. Measles. The epidemic has swept through Stones Creek beginning in late February. Several adults and children, including a woman living in Sanctuary House, had died. The town was still recovering from the losses.

"Don't rightly care just now. I got me a new woman, and I'm fixin' on trying her out." The man, Ornan, took a step toward Gema.

"Nyet." Gema jumped up and began running. He caught her within four steps. She began swinging her fists, clipping him on the jaw.

Ornan smacked her across the cheek. "You'll learn to do as you're told."

"Ornan," the woman said. She strode to where they were and jerked his hand from Gema's arm. "Can't you see she's scared to death? She might not even be able to understand what you say. She's speakin' some foreign language. If you take her now, she'll not accept her lot. She'll fight you and you'll never be able to turn your back on her.

"Remember Edna? You all took her too soon, and she nearly killed Phil, over there." She pointed at another man.

There was a jagged scar running down his face. "She stabbed Fred too. Then, you all beat her and left her. Lot of good it did you to grab her and use her right away."

Ornan studied Gema. She flinched back when he reached out. "You gotta point." He looked at the other men. "How about we wait a couple of days. Three at most. Get her used to being here. Then, we'll make sure she understands her place real well."

There were grumbles, but the men were nodding as they did so.

Ornan grabbed Gema's arm again and jerked her to him. He landed a sour breathed kiss on her mouth then shoved her toward the woman. "That's just a sweet taste for your pleasure. I'll get mine later." He looked at the woman who stared back at him. "Take her into the cave. We men have got some planning to do." He turned and walked back to the men. They moved to a grouping of logs set around a fire pit.

"Come." The woman motioned to Gema who glanced back at the men, then followed her into the cave.

The space was large enough not to be crowded. There were three fire pits. Pallets were scattered around with blankets, and a few had pillows. Saddle bags, food, and other supplies were in piles. There was a water barrel near the entrance. Nothing was clean or efficiently arranged. And the place smelled. Urine, feces, and vomit fought for dominance.

From the dim light of the fires, Gema could see a couple of children lying on pallets. The ones who had come to the cave opening retreated to lie down on others.

"I'm Flora," the woman said. "What's your name? Can you understand me?"

"Gema. I, Gema." The words were said barely above a whisper. She couldn't force more strength into them.

"Come and sit." Flora led her to a log near the fire. She went to the water barrel and dipped the ladle in, then brought it to Gema. "Drink."

Gema obeyed the command.

"Where's they steal you from?"

"Stones Creek."

Flora swore. "Them idiots. They had to go to a town that has a sheriff who knows what he's doing." She began pacing.

Another woman approached and held out a piece of dried meat and a tin cup with beans. Gema took them and spooned some beans into her mouth. They were tasteless, but she knew she had to eat.

"I'm Sally." She placed a cup of coffee next to Gema. She moved away and crouched down on the other side of the fire.

Someone started coughing. Sally moved to a pallet and picked up a child whose long hair seemed to indicate it was a girl. When she came back to the fire, Gema could see that the little one had the measles. She was small and thin, with a dirty face covered in a red rash. Her eyes were swollen and watery.

Another child, a boy somewhat older came over and sat next to Sally. He leaned against her. He looked to be about eight. In the firelight, Gema couldn't tell whether he was coming down with the measles or recovering. The rash on his face was lighter than on the girl's.

Flora paced back and stood in front of Gema. "You're going to leave. I'm not sure how, but you aren't staying here. I'm not going to be party to another woman's abuse by the likes of these men.

"When Lloyd was leader, he put a stop to the kidnappings. He's dead. Ornan has started them up again." She looked over Gema's shoulder focusing on the wall behind her. "Chloe got out. I thought she'd died back in Minnesota where we abandoned her. I felt so awful when Buster King did that. She was so close to giving birth." Flora turned her gaze onto Gema again. "I didn't know she was still alive until I heard Buster say she was living in Stones Creek. That gave me hope. Hope that maybe someday I can get out."

Flora squatted down and looked Gema in the eye. "I'm gonna do whatever it takes to give you the chance to get outta here. You're gonna take it, you hear? You're gonna grab the chance and run as fast and far as you can. Don't think about any of us. We know what to do. How to live."

Sally came over and placed a hand on Flora's shoulder. "What are you gonna do?"

Flora looked up. "What do you think? I'm gonna give them a distraction so Gema, here, can get away."

Gema found her voice, words in English. "What kind distraction?"

"Only two things will draw their attention and the first will just point them back to you. So I'll get 'em good and drunk." Flora stood and marched over to a pile of supplies and pulled out several jugs. She came back, looked at Gema, then Sally. "You be sure to get her out of here."

~~~~~

Red Dickerson rode Ralph up the hill into the forest. He'd been on the far end of the ranch for several weeks, ever since his betrothal to Laura Duffle had ended. The owner, Hawk Connor, had given him permission to come up to the line shack and look for stray cows and calves even though he was the foreman of Hawk's Wing Ranch.

He'd also tasked Red with keeping an eye out for the gang of outlaws who were terrorizing the region. Two, the leader Buster King and his brother had been captured late last year when they attempted to kidnap one of the House ladies from the café where she worked. Since then, the rest of the gang had killed a settler and burned the homestead and barn. So far, they'd proven illusive. This remote area had several caves and plenty of water from the streams that ran down from the mountains.

Red was living in the shack and riding the hills and plains daily. He was doing a lot of thinking too. He'd messed up with Laura, and she'd given him the mitten. He wasn't that upset as they'd truly only been friends.

What bothered him more was that he now had to figure out where and how to find another woman he could be interested in enough to marry. He'd already eliminated each of the women of Sanctuary House.

Last summer eight women and their children had come to Stones Creek to live in the house Nugget Nate Ryder, the millionaire mountain man, had built. He had a mission for women in need back in Iowa called Sanctuary Place. Red had heard the stories of Nate having Callings from God to go to specific places. There, he found women who had fallen into hard times of their own making or that were thrust upon them. They were supported and given schooling, training, and especially the message that God so loved them that He gave His only Son for them.

With the dire shortage of women in the West, Nate had built Sanctuary House so the women of his mission could move to Stones Creek with the possibility of finding a husband. To safeguard the women and their children, Nate had given four town leaders the obligation of approving each man before he could court one of the women. Only three of the original women were still unmarried.

In January, two more ladies had come. Libby Trembly and Gema Volko-something. Neither of them had children, which was appealing, but Red had been involved with courting Laura at the time. Libby had a sadness about her that Red didn't think he'd ever be able to breach. Gema was young, only twenty. At thirty-four, Red thought she was too young for him.

Well, maybe if another batch of women came this summer he'd find one he wanted to court. He'd be sure to watch his tongue next time.

Rain had begun falling about a half an hour before and with the temperature dropping it was beginning to turn into sleet. Red was thankful he'd bought one of the new hats Ben Cutler was selling in his store. It was made by an eastern company called Stetson. Wide-brimmed and made of felted fur, the hat was expensive but looked as though it would last him a lifetime. It kept the sun out of his eyes and was now keeping the rain and sleet from slipping past his collar and down his back.

A flash of white appeared between the trees. Not the white you'd see on a cow. No, it was more the white of a shirt.

Red kicked his horse into a gallop. He studied the area as he approached, slowing Ralph to a walk. Hawk had warned him not to try to take on the outlaws. All he was going to do was scout and see if he could tell where their hideout might be.

The white darted between trees again. Yellow trailed behind. Not yellow cloth, blond hair. Long blond hair. Whoever it was had long hair and was probably a woman. Red kicked Ralph's side again, speeding him up. A woman out here in the rain and sleet was in danger whether she was part of the outlaw gang or not.

As Red moved closer he got a better glimpse of the woman. His jaw dropped, and he almost did the same to the reins. That was Gema Volko-something. Her Russian name always escaped him, not that he could pronounce it anyway. What was she doing this far from Stones Creek? Without a coat. The day had started off warm for late March, but the weather was fickle, and the temperature was dropping fast.

Gema looked behind her for a second and screamed. She ran even faster, dodging between the trees. Red called her name, hoping she'd recognize his voice. She just kept running.

Then, she went down, falling into a small stream that cut its way down the hillside. Red caught up just as she was trying to get up. Her skirts were soaked, making it difficult for her to rises.

Red jumped off Ralph and ran to her, pulling her from the stream. Gema screamed and fought him, wind milling her arms, trying to hit him with her fists. He grabbed her hands, bringing her to his chest. He wrapped his arms around her, hoping to stop her struggles.

"Shh, Gema, it's Red Dickerson. You're safe with me. Shh." He kept up what he hoped were comforting words and sounds. He didn't know if she was understanding him in her panic. Finally, she stopped and looked up at him. Recognition seeped into her being. Gema laid her head on his chest and began to cry. She was trembling. Red didn't know whether it was from the cold and wet or panic. He did know he had to get her out of the rain and into warm, dry clothing.

"Come, let's get away from here. When you're warm and dry, you can tell me why you are way out here." He led her over to Ralph. "Stand here while I mount. Then, I'll lift you up." He hugged her once before letting her go. "You're safe with me."

Red mounted then reached down to lift her onto the saddle in front of him. There was no way, in her condition, that she could hold on to his waist or the back of the saddle. She was shaking too hard. By placing her in front he could tuck her into his coat, sharing his warmth with her.

Soon, he had her settled against him, knowing she was as secure and protected as he could provide."Hup," he said. Red kicked Ralph's side and turned the horse toward the line shack.